COSMO

A DRAGON VEIL UNIVERSE NOVEL

DRAGON GUARDIANS
BOOK ONE

MINERVA HOWE

DRAGON VEIL UNIVERSE

Dragon Hoard
> Dragon Scholar
> Dragon Collector
> Dragon Treasure

Dragon Prophecy
> Mist Dragon
> Cloud Dragon
> Shadow Dragon

Dragon Sanctuary
> Winter Dragon
> Ice Dragon
> Frost Dragon
> Snow Dragon
> Frozen Dragon

Misunderstood
> Wolven Winter
> Shifting Winter

Healing Winter

Solitary Dragons
Archer
Aiden
Devlin

To Nita D. who is always so supportive and, as always, to my wife BA.

For Alex, Jason, Jaymi, Michael, and my Patreon beta crew who make me look better than I am.

ONE

"Hey, guys. Check this out." Corbin called him and Cullen over, so Cosmo dutifully went with it, leaving his paintbrush balanced on the can of purple paint he was using to coat the gate. He loved the southwest tradition of using that color to ward off evil spirits, and he figured Pagosa Springs qualified as southwest.

Right?

"What's up, bro?" Cosmo asked, coming to peer over Corbin's shoulder. Or around it. The jolly fucking green giant was hard to see over. They might be triplets, but he was pretty sure they were fraternal. One way or the other, Corbin took after their dad.

"I'm growing gooseberries, raspberries, and wild strawberries."

"Yay. That bodes well for jelly in late summer, hmm?" And mixed berry pies. He did love those. Or cobblers. Uhn.

"It does." Corbin beamed at him. And we'll have rose hips too. For tea and jelly. This place is really amazing. I mean, it's been abandoned for a bit, but the plants and soil were just waiting for someone to come along and love them again." Corbin turned back to his plants, waving his hands at them.

"Cool." He felt that way about the house proper. It went deep into the mountain now, and there was a way, if one knew how, to get to the land across the veil, both the dragon dimension of Lunastra and the Land of Summer.

And since he and his brothers were both half dragon and half fae... Well, this house was the perfect gateway between all the worlds. This was their place. Their calling.

"Neat." Cullen flicked a hand and an illusion of a shower of rose petals floated through the air. "I love rose hip jelly."

Cosmo chuckled and shook his head, swallowing his jealousy. He had skills, sure, but they weren't as impressive as Cullen's. "Show off."

"For all the good it's done me," Cullen scoffed.

He shook his head. "Your damn illusion talent has saved our bacon more than once." Not too long ago, they'd all worked for an alpha dragon named Gavin, doing rescue for dragons and other folks who needed their special skills. And Cullen's talent came in very, very handy. Way more in that profession than his and Corbin's.

"Yeah. It's weird, isn't it? Being...here?" Cullen had been the one that was most worried about ending up in the Halloran house. This house had a reputation.

Dragons had died here.

Been murdered here.

It was more than a little "weird."

"It's our job to make it not strange," Corbin said, stroking the leaves of a plant, which rose up toward his touch. "And you guys are doing amazing on the house and the porches and all. I love the purple."

"We're trying." They had also called upon Lady Arian to come and bless the house, to clear some of the energy in it.

"Mmm." Cullen shrugged, looking dubious. "There are still a few rooms I don't love."

"Then they need more cleansing. Cosmo?" Corbin looked at him.

"Yeah. I'll have to see what I can do…" He wasn't the best at this, but he had a little talent in his own way, and he was awfully available.

"Cool. That's settled then." Corbin turned back to his plants, and Cosmo chuckled, moving over to pick up his paintbrush.

The moment he touched it to the gate, he felt the lightning sensation running up his arms and into his brain that meant he was about to have a vision. Crap. He opened his mouth, but nothing came out, and he knew he was going down.

This was a doozy.

A huge black shadow covered the sky, a streak of fire splitting the air and setting the world alight. He ducked, knowing if that fire touched him it would burn him alive.

He tried to call a warning to his brothers, but nothing would come out. Just white noise.

He shook his head, wanting to ward it off by running into the house, but something kept pulling him toward the sky.

There was nothing he could do, nothing at all. The dragon was reaching for him, the huge beast relentless, claws outstretched.

"Cosmo!" Corbin's big, booming voice reached him through the fog, those hard hands on his shoulders. "I got you, bro. Come on. You're scaring us."

He snapped back to the present, choking on his own spit a little.

"What the hell?" Cullen asked him. "You were foaming."

He shook his head, trying desperately to warn them, to breathe, but he couldn't quite make his brain work.

"Inside," Corbin barked, and Cullen helped lift him and carry him in, wrapping him in a blanket so he could stretch out on the couch. His lips felt numb. Who was that and why was he, because it was a big male alpha dragon, no doubt, after them?

"Brother. Brother, we're good. We're good. Don't panic, please." Cullen sounded worried, like he was panicked himself.

He sucked in a deep breath, then let it out. "I saw a huge male dragon. He was flying over the house, and I felt this pull, as if he was trying to get us to come out so he could flame us."

"It was a fire dragon?" Corbin asked.

"Yes. A giant one. Old. Older than Gavin, maybe."

"Why would he come after us?" Cullen asked.

"Because we guard the veil?"

"It could be, but no one knows we're here yet, right? Just the clutch." Corbin waved toward the hallway that led to Lunastra and Gavin and Austin and Dustin and all the babies. "They won't harm us."

"No. No, but what if someone thought they were going to get across the veil, and he didn't?" He wrapped his arms around himself as he sat up. "What if someone was pissed?"

"No way. If someone is still here, it's for a reason. That means they have no real reason to come after us." That was Cullen.

"Okay, then why was he spitting fire in my vision?"

Corbin shrugged. "Heartburn?"

"Melting snow," Cullen offered.

"Uh...he was boiling water for tea?"

"Could be smelting."

Cosmo arched an eyebrow. "Smelting."

"Ore. For his hoard."

"You don't tend to do that in the air," Cosmo said drily. But the image did make him laugh.

"No, but who knows?" Cullen put a hand on his arm. "It was just me talking about the house being weird. That's all."

"I bet." But he wanted to get out there and finish painting his gate. "Can someone get me a Coke? The sugar will do me good."

"Totally. We had a bunch of supplies delivered today— including snacks for the dragons." Corbin shook his head. "They do love Doritos."

"They really do." Cullen chuckled, going to grab him a Coke, bringing it to him. "Here, bro. Sugar and bubbles."

"Two of my favorite things!" Better than visions, that was for damn sure.

"Mine too!" Cullen sat next to him after shoving his feet off the couch. He also had a Coke, and Corbin brought some Oreos for them all to share. He snuggled into his brothers, letting their nearness comfort him.

He loved times like this, where they could all sit and be together and support each other. No rivalry, none of the weirdness of the last few years in their worlds. So much magic, and it had needed somewhere to go, so it had crossed the veil into other realms.

Which was why he didn't understand his vision.

Everything had changed again, but they were dealing

with it as a family, and they—well, they had their own home. And it was a grand one. A cabin slash A-frame slash Victorian that had sort of grown up and together organically and that went deep into the mountain.

Cosmo loved it.

And he'd remade his little den, his bower, to be so reflective of him. It was full of Victorian floral wallpaper on a deep green background, a huge bed with hangings that kept the cold out and the secrecy in. Pillows and tassels and books and Regency tables and bookshelves that hid a secret room...

He adored it.

He took a cookie from Corbin. "Anyway, it doesn't matter. It was just a vision. Right? Half the time, they don't mean anything."

"And half the time they mean an apocalypse," Cullen muttered.

"Mmm." *Gee thanks, bro.*

You're welcome. Cullen winked at him, and he rolled his eyes. Ah. Family. They were assholes, but he was so glad they were here.

His particular talent was a lonely one at best. If he had to go it alone, he would be certifiable by now.

CHAPTER

TWO

Hawk Fitzhugh settled on the heights between Wolf Creek Pass and Pagosa Springs. He'd done several flyovers at night, but he needed to view the house during the day.

Thankfully, he had excellent long-range vision. Not so helpful was the fact that his dragon magic eyes made it impossible to pass as human. Good thing some kindly soul had invented dark sunglasses.

He'd missed the opening of the veil by several months. He wasn't sure how long. But it was nearly the summer solstice now, and he'd been...traveling.

Before the veil had opened and closed, he'd been hibernating. He'd been asleep for nearly two decades, the human world moving too fast for him. But he'd awakened in a cave, his house just...gone.

He wasn't certain what magic that had been, but it had happened. And then Hawk had felt the tug. The call to go East, of all things, leaving his Northern California aerie for Colorado.

The house sat in splendid isolation, the magic signature

throbbing from it. It was unique—part cabin, part A-frame, part *his* house.

No question.

That stained-glass tower window was handmade by him.

How had it come to be here? He would never believe someone had stolen it. Not in any real way. Magic could be amazing, but that kind of malfeasance would have awakened him. An angry mob always had, for instance. Long before the mob had reached him.

This felt...natural.

As if his house belonged there.

People were living in the house. He saw smoke, doors opening and closing, and movement in a garden that was utterly breathtaking.

He couldn't make out a lot of details, which was odd. Because whoever it was down there made his heart pound. Made his whole body buzz. That was—It was a hell of a sensation. And not a familiar one. He peered closer, trying to sharpen his vision. He couldn't just fly down there; not at this time of day. Even if he cloaked himself in shadows, he would cast a shadow.

He saw a figure appear at the top of the cupola, and for a moment, he swore eyes were resting on him.

Impossible. He was hidden in the trees, and he was camouflaged as well. There was no way someone that far down could see him no matter who they were.

But maybe he called to them as they did him.

That wasn't the strangest idea ever. His home wasn't going to allow just anyone in his house. Maybe he knew them somehow, though his gut told him no.

And his gut was rarely wrong.

So he stared, trying to make out anything that he could while he fought the urge to take to the sky.

For a half a heartbeat, he smelled roses.

His nose worked, and he looked around, but there was nary a rose up here. No, this was from that house down there. So it was time to work his way down there. In a stealthy way.

He didn't love stealth.

He was gigantic.

Black-scaled.

With eyes that looked like faceted stones.

Not inconspicuous.

But he wanted to be down there before nightfall. So he would bundle up and head down on foot. He could chug along pretty quickly, and there weren't too many people if he stayed off the road.

If he was lucky, he could stay close to the land, moving good and fast toward the house that glowed in his sight.

He wasn't one to suffer from curiosity too long. No, he liked to know what was what. And why he'd had to steal clothes on his way out of California because everything else in his home was gone.

He raced down the mountain, avoiding the cars and the tourists who had stopped to take pictures. Great heights scared humans, and they felt good about making it over the pass...

The person who was in the cupola—were those wings?

Were there dragons in his house?

His heart started to pound again. He wasn't sure if he was excited, furious, or terrified. It had been...an eon since he'd seen another dragon.

He kept moving, the house backlit by the settling sun, causing it to glow, almost to shine. It called to him, and he slid into the yard area just as the sun was going down, careful to blend with the shadows of the trees.

There were masses of roses and berry bushes and columbines, and he could see vegetable sprouts out back. The gate was purple, the front door turquoise blue. It was lovely.

He felt like an intruder. Like he should leave.

The door opened, and he blinked as a purple young man who was wearing a most life-like bear stood there. "Rawr."

"Hello, brother bear," Hawk said, honoring the illusion. "I am sorry to bother you. Can you tell me why my house is here?"

The big head tilted, and then a slender young man stood before him. "Corbin! Cosmo! You better come."

He blinked. There was more than one, which explained why he knew this wasn't the one he'd seen up in the tower.

"Get back in the house, brother." This man was larger, green, hands over his chest. "Can I help you?"

"I hope so." He kept it polite rather than roaring. He jerked his chin to the tower. "That's my house."

"This is the old Halloran place. The last surviving brother asked us to guard it."

"Yes, but how much of it?" He waved a hand. "That turret, cupola, and stained-glass window is mine."

"How could it be yours? It was in Myk's family for over one hundred years." The soft voice made him blink, want to roar.

Hawk smelled roses.

"Well, I built it over two hundred years ago." He shook his head. "I'm afraid I have no pictures. I woke up in a cave."

"Let him in, Corbin. It's dark, and we need to make supper."

"But—"

"Corbin."

"Fine!" The green one sighed loudly and stepped back to allow him inside.

"Thank you?" This didn't look like his home at all. The foyer was all cabin, and it went through to an A-frame on one side that was all glass. It went back into a hall that maybe went into the mountain.

"So you're from here? Did you know the Hallorans?" That was the purple one. How...colorful.

"No. I have been in Northern California for a long time." He looked around, taking in the scents and sights.

"Um...this is Colorado?"

Like he didn't know that. "I understand where I am, Rosie."

"Rosie?" The young one scowled at him.

"That is your color." And his scent.

"My name is Cosmo. Do you eat steak?"

He blinked some more. "Of course I do. I'm a dragon." They were carnivores. Well. Omnivores, but meat was essential at their size.

"We're eating in the courtyard. Come on in." That was green and grumpy, the man all scowls.

"Thank you." He was suddenly starving, not sure when he had eaten last. One got accustomed to not having to hunt...

"No problem. Do you have a name?" Rosie asked. "It's weird to just call you 'new guy'."

"Hawk Fitzhugh."

"Mr. Fitzhugh." Rosie winked at him.

"Don't you mean bird brain?"

He growled softly. "What, Grizzly?"

That had the dragon giggling hard.

The green sprout rolled his eyes. "I'm getting a headache."

"Everything gives you a headache," the purple one said.

"And I assume you also have names?" Hawk asked politely.

"I'm Cullen," Violets dropped from Cullen's hand onto the floor. "This is my big brother Corbin, and the one you called Rosie is Cosmo."

He arrowed his gaze in on Cosmo. "You are very…pink."

"And you look like you were baked in lava."

"Thank you." He was forged in fire, as it were. He inclined his head. "Are you an illusion dragon as well?"

"No. Cullen takes after our father, and Corbin after our mother."

He tilted his head. "And you? Who do you resemble?"

Cosmo scoffed. "I think I'm a changeling."

Cullen rolled his eyes. "We're triplets."

"That means nothing and you know it."

"He's just grumpy because he's a seer. That's hard. Sometimes there's foam."

"Oh. A seer." He bowed deeply. "This is important. Are you also a scribe?"

"Can I write? Absolutely. I keep a journal even."

"Ah." He nodded. Yes. It was important to illuminate prophecies and portents. This one must be protected. That was no doubt why he was meant to be here. The brothers would find mates and the seer would be alone.

"Steaks, right? That's it? Steaks?" Cosmo offered him a smile, and Corbin groaned.

"Steaks. Come on."

"I will love that." And he followed, like Alice down the rabbit hole. He had no idea what to expect, but he would be delighted to see where this went.

THREE

Did we just invite a big dragon in?
What if he's a bad guy?
What if he sets the house on fire?
Should we go call Gavin?
Should we drug his steak?
Do drugs work on dragons?

Cosmo and Cullen stared at each other, fretting in unison.

Corbin just cooked steaks. Doggedly. Ignoring them all.

And the big guy with scales like polished obsidian looked so beautiful he hurt. His faceted eyes, no longer hidden behind tinted lenses, gleamed red and gold, and he was probably stunning all shifted out. He looked almost human, but kind of like a video game character in armor like this. As if he didn't quite know how to be human but he was trying to blend in.

And his clothes...

They were ill-fitted and weird, as if he'd stolen them from a dozen clotheslines. Maybe he had. He said he'd woke up in a cave with no house...

Or maybe he was just insane. Either way, what bliss. Cosmo had no idea what to do. How to take this all.

It's a little exciting, though, he admitted. *And he's crazy hot.*

Cullen glanced at him. *You think so?*

Uh-huh.

Weird.

His cheeks heated, and he shrugged. He really did think Hawk was...whoa.

It didn't matter. It was just the truth.

It's okay. It's been a long time since we had a hookup. Cullen rolled his eyes. *You're glowing.*

Stop it!

Corbin rumbled. *Both of you quit it. Right now.*

He stuck out his tongue but pulled it back in hurriedly when Hawk glanced at him, expression curious.

Cosmo ducked his head and headed over to "help" Corbin with the steaks.

Cullen threw together some kind of side. It would either be a salad or coleslaw, and then garlic bread. He wasn't a particularly creative cook. In fact, that usually fell to Cosmo.

Cosmo just found himself weirdly unable to *do* anything. Except dither.

Go sit and talk to him. Corbin shoved him toward Hawk.

What? Me? Why?

Stop it.

He nodded and then shook his head.

"Are you well, little rose?" Hawk asked, concern edging out the curiosity.

"I am. Sorry. I'm a little—You're our first company. Usually, we are the ones visiting."

"Ah." Hawk said that a lot. He propped his chin on his hand. "Who do you visit? Family?"

"Our clutch, yes. They are...close."

"I see." He thought Hawk seemed almost...disappointed.

"Do you have a clutch?"

"No. I grew up alone."

"We've never been alone." They had grown up in the Land of Summer, only going to explore the human world as adults.

"No, no, I can tell."

Cosmo wasn't sure what that meant, but it didn't seem an insult...

It was just the truth, he supposed.

"Here we go. Steaks and...stuff."

"I made baked potatoes earlier," Cullin said. "So salad and potatoes."

"It smells amazing," Hawk said.

"Well, hopefully it is..."

"We don't entertain much..."

"We don't need to."

"I'm sorry." Hawk looked at them all in turn. "I don't mean to intrude, but I need to know what's happening."

Cosmo tilted his head. "With what?"

Corbin wrung his hands. *Should we call Gavin?*

Maybe? We can't just ask him about everything. Cullen shook his head.

Why not? Hell, he's an elder dragon. Maybe he knows this guy.

"With my house. I assume I missed the veil opening. I was asleep."

"It did, yes. It just all happened recently." And that was awful, to have just missed it.

"Yes, well, I can understand that. But my house disappeared, and I did not."

"It was Myk's family's house for a long, long time..." And it was his now, and it was going to suck if he lost it.

That got him a faint smile. "Only part of it is mine..."

"Only Cosmo's part! That's not fair. We didn't know!" Corbin stood at his shoulder.

Hawk studied him, those wild eyes so...cool. "I see."

"We...let's eat. It's not like we're going to make you stay outside. You need help."

"I could use some, yes. But I have no intention of taking away your things or your home."

"Well, then." Cosmo held out his hand. "Welcome, friend dragon, I'm Cosmo. Let's have some steak."

Hawk took his hand, and it was as if lightning shot through him, electrifying his whole body. He gasped, and Hawk's eyes widened.

"Yes," Hawk said. "Let's."

Hawk's mouth fell open when Cosmo touched him, because he'd never felt anything like it. It was... concentrated fire. It was prophecy come to life.

It was truth.

He wanted to keep touching Cosmo.

Cosmo gasped, staring at him. "Dragon. Dragon. Dragon. Dragon."

"I—" He held onto Cosmo, his body shivering.

"Hey. Guys? Steak. What the heck?"

The lavender brother's eyes went wide. "He's having a vision, Cor!"

"No!" Cosmo shook his head. "I mean—"

"Shh." He stroked Cosmo's hand with his thumb. "All is well. I promise."

"Yes. You're hungry. I should feed you. I need to feed you."

"Please." He beamed at Cosmo. "We should eat together, Rosie."

"Strangeness..." Corbin sighed and shook his head. "So much strangeness."

"No shit, Cor." The other one handed out silverware, then dug into his meal.

He couldn't stop staring at Cosmo.

Those eyes were sapphire and sparkling, dark and amazing. They were stunning and focused on him.

"After steak, perhaps you could show me your part of the house?" he asked. He wanted to see, but he also wanted to be alone with Cosmo. Badly.

"I think that's a terrible idea," Corbin put in.

"What? He's going to put it back on the West Coast?" Cosmo asked. "For fuck's sake, it's trapped where it is now. It's not going anywhere."

He just cut a piece of steak, which was beautifully cooked, and had a bite. He was hungry. Very much so. It just never seemed prudent to let someone know how bad off you had been... And it was lovely to hear Cosmo defend him.

"I would just like to see," he put in mildly.

"We'll all go! We're still pretty new. We love exploring. This place has ghosts, but it has magic as well." Cullen waved his hand, sending rainbow sparkles about.

"Of course." Disappointment speared him, and Cosmo's face took on a mutinous expression, but no one argued.

It would do no good, Hawk could tell.

Regardless, this was still the most fun he'd had in decades. Perhaps longer.

"I hope your hoard is here. Do you think it is?" Cullen blinked at him.

Corbin shook his head. "Right now, we need to see if we can find him clothes and shoes."

"And comfy things for his private parts."

Cosmo made him smile.

Are you worried about my private parts, Rosie?

Cosmo blinked up at him, wide-eyed. "And about your hoard. I haven't seen it."

Nice save. But his hoard was a large one... All precious stones, and all one-color variation. Tourmaline. Pink sapphires. Pink topaz. Rose quartz and pink diamonds...

He understood the obsession now... He'd been waiting.

He'd been waiting, and Cosmo was here.

In his house.

Hawk smiled, knowing now why he hadn't crossed the veil.

His life was about to start again.

"My hoard is safe here. I have no doubt." He didn't have to doubt. Cosmo was protecting it. He might not know it yet... But there it was.

"It is. I mean, if it's in the house somewhere, no one is getting to it." Cosmo smiled at him, cheeks darkening a bit.

They ate in silence for a bit, all of them polishing off their steaks. Then Cosmo hopped up. "Come see my part of the house."

"Of course." He rose, following.

The scent of Cosmo was heavenly, and he barely resisted the urge to touch. As it was, he grazed Cosmo's back with his fingers, just barely.

Tingles. You can hear me, can't you? I've never heard anyone but my brothers. You can hear me. You can hear me.

I can hear you, my sweet rose. Excitement filled him, starting at his toes and rising like the lava he'd been accused of breathing more than once. Really, it was more like he spit it.

Cosmo's excitement felt like tingles, dragging up and down his spine. He understood. He felt energized. Interested. For the first time in ages.

"So this is the main part of the house. We've got a couple of rooms blocked off, because they're...haunted." Cullen sighed softly.

"Haunted?" His eyebrows rose up. "By whom?"

Corbin shook his head, shaggy green hair like a mane. "A family of dragons were murdered here. One male omega and three children survived."

Vampires. It was vampires.

Oh. That made him angry on their behalf. *Vampires are unnatural.*

They fed on the babies. They almost killed them and Myk.

He wanted to roar about that. *No. Not babies. Are they dead?*

The babies are alive. The vamps are dead, but this was the house they came to...

That's horrid. He would have hunted the vamps down and killed them if no one else had. Thankfully, he didn't have to leave Cosmo.

Cosmo nodded. *Say, "It's stunning."*

He blinked, then opened his mouth. "It's stunning."

Cullen beamed. "Thanks! I think we did a great job painting it."

"Absolutely." *Thank you, sweet Rosie.*

Any time.

"Now, this is the stairway to the tower." That was Corbin.

"I know." He squatted down, then ran his hand over the lower step. "Here are my marks where I signed when I made them."

"Oh wow!" That was all three triplets, who immediately came to see.

He smiled. His mark was a carved Hawk, one that might pass for a dragon if one looked closely enough.

It meant a lot that they were willing to listen, to believe he was who he said he was. And he was. How this had happened was a mystery, but the why...

Cosmo.

I love your mark—it's perfect. Cosmo touched his hand, the touch featherlight.

Thank you, love. I like it. I've used it since... Hawk frowned. *For a very long time.* He couldn't remember how long. He'd been born on the other side of the veil. Being cast out had hurt his memory. So had all the many years of living on the human plane.

Cosmo made a soft noise of sympathy.

"You okay, bro?" Cullen asked.

"Fine. I think this is just hard on Hawk, hmm?" Cosmo stroked his arm, and his energy levels seemed to spark.

"It's been a tiring couple of days." Hawk just tried to smile.

"Would you like to lie down a bit?"

Only if you come with me...

Cosmo flushed dark again. *I can't yet. The brothers will want to talk about you being here.*

"May I bathe?" Hawk asked aloud. "I would love that." In fact, he would dearly love to wallow in a bath.

"Of course you can! There's a huge tub."

"Yes, with pink tiles."

Like it was meant for me. Like it was built just for me.

I think it was, my love. I can't wait for you to see my hoard.
"Thank you, my friends. I appreciate it. I will clean up after myself."

"I should have some clothes that will fit you," Corbin said. "I take way more after dad."

"Is he the dragon?"

"Yes. Mom is fae."

"I thought that must be the case. Your eyes give you away. So pretty, all of you."

Cosmo blushed, and Cullen laughed for him.

"Come on, Cos. You can take him his clothes." Corbin's gaze was absolutely firm.

"Okay." Cosmo gave him one more lingering gaze, then left him with Cullen, who showed him to the bathroom.

"Cosmo will be back in a bit. The water gets hot."

"I like heat." He could fly into a volcano... Literally.

"Well, just be careful." Cullen waved him into the bathroom, then left him.

He looked around after he turned on the lights, curious to see what was the same and what was different. There was a slightly more romantic Victorian touch to the room now, the walls still green above the pink tile, but the fixtures more...frilly. The lights less terrifying and old.

The towels were thick and luxurious, and there was a heavy curtain of material to draw around the tub—for privacy? Heat retention?

Whatever it was, he liked it. He rubbed the fabric between his fingers, loving how it wasn't strange and plastic. It was heavy, luxurious. No doubt it would shed water like a duck, but it was still very lush.

He started the water, amazed as always at how hot

water just gushed out of a pipe. Running water had been about for a long while, but heated like this? Without a bucket or a brazier?

Such a marvel. Like his own personal hot springs.

He stripped and settled in, peeping as the cold tub touched his back. The chill didn't last long, though, the hot water seeping around to warm him.

Oh, this was heaven.

He wiggled his toes, smiling at them. Dirty. Ugh.

Hawk could see hints of Cosmo everywhere in here—colorful clothes, a couple of books, a pile of candles in the window box.

He breathed in deeply, and yes, he could smell that rose and sandalwood scent too. There was also a deep hint of musk, something that spoke of how Cosmo touched himself when he was in here.

His cock twitched in a hopeful sort of way.

It had been so long. So long, and Cosmo awakened sensations he hadn't felt in eons. If he were honest, he'd never felt anything like Cosmo made him feel. He had a deep want within him now. A wild excitement.

Hunger.

This was actual hunger, and he welcomed it.

He hummed, then found the yummy-scented soap that Cosmo kept by the tub and scrubbed up a bit. He wanted to smell nice just in case he could convince Cosmo to sneak off with him and indulge in some kissing. Or more. And this way, he wouldn't make wherever they let him sleep smell like a cave.

I've got some clothes for you. Where should I leave them? Oh, his Cosmo.

You can bring them in, if you like. I didn't lock it. Would that lure Cosmo inside to him? He hoped so.

The doorknob turned, and Cosmo slid inside, closing the door behind him, arms filled with clothes. "Hey."

"Hello." He lifted his toes again, this time to wave at Cosmo. "This is very comfy."

"It is. I like it very much." Cosmo perched on a little tufted bench.

"It smells like you, sweet. That makes it even better." He wanted to sleep in Cosmo's bed with him.

"Does it? I'm glad. I didn't know what kinds of clothes you liked, so...we just brought a bunch. Soft."

"Thank you. I'm sure it will be fine. Even if mine are here, they will be sorely out of fashion." He had a feeling he'd slept longer than he supposed.

"I haven't found any of your clothes, but we're still exploring. We've been—working hard to make this a safe space."

"Of course. That's okay." He was really more worried about his rocks. And his books. He had a few very special ones in Old Dragon.

"I'm sorry that I took your house. Myk gave it to us." Cosmo twisted a napkin in his fingers.

"You didn't take it, Cosmo." He shook his head, rinsing off. He'd offer to let Cosmo join him, but the water was dirty.

"No, but still..." Cosmo stood and brought him a fluffy towel.

"Thank you." He rose as well, letting the water drain, then turning it on to splash some on him to rinse off.

Cosmo watched him openly, tongue sliding over his lips.

He wanted to reach for Cosmo, but he thought the brothers might show up soon. He heard stealthy footsteps.

Cosmo nodded to him. *It's not fair. They think you've glamoured me. Have you?*

No, love. I haven't. Your Cullen should know that. He's the illusion one, yes? I don't have that kind of magic. I can cloak myself well enough when I fly. I can spit lava at an enemy. I'm a throwback.

You're amazing. I dreamed—The thought broke off, but he saw a glimpse of the vision, a huge dragon circling the house.

Yes. I was doing reconnaissance. He chuckled. *I watched from the heights, too.* And then he'd actually seen Cosmo on the tower, and he'd been unable to resist coming all the way down to the ground level and finding out what was what.

"I wasn't scared, much. You know I'm not a full dragon, don't you?" Cosmo brought him a pair of soft pants, helping him dress with gentle, warm hands.

"I do. You are part fae, yes?" He reached out to rub a hand over Cosmo's hair, unable to resist. Oh, it was soft and lovely, and he smiled at the feel of it.

"Yes. My mother is a Blessed one." Cosmo smiled and stepped closer. "Oh dragon..."

A sharp knock came to the door, and Cosmo rolled his eyes. "Cos? Brother? Both of you okay?"

"We're fine."

"Okay. We just wondered."

Cosmo mouthed, "Go away," and he chuckled again.

"We should go on out and appease them. There will be time later."

"Yeah. They're not going to be decent until we do." Cosmo rolled his eyes. "Brothers."

"You love them very much. I can tell."

"Well, sure. I have no idea what I would do without them. But right now, they could get lost."

"That is not fun. I've been that way for too long."

"Oh, dragon, that's just a saying, not a wish."

"Is it?" He frowned. "Hmm. Meaning they could leave you alone?"

"Bingo!" Cosmo laughed, but it was for him, not at him.

"Bingo is a game. I remember that, I believe." Goodness, so much to learn. He hugged Cosmo gently before they left the bathroom, as thanks, mainly.

It shocked him when Cosmo wrapped lean, surprisingly strong arms around him, and squeezed him tight.

He leaned for a moment, smelling Cosmo's hair, feeling how warm and wonderful Cosmo was against him.

"Okay, that's enough. Out. No nookie with a dragon you just met!" Corbin banged on the door.

"I'm not nookie-ing. I'm hugging." Cosmo sounded outraged.

He patted Cosmo's butt, the familiarity making him so happy. "We're coming. He was helping me figure out these ingenious pants." He didn't want to get Cosmo in trouble with his family. He could take it slowly.

For now.

FOUR

Cosmo was going to hit his brothers in the head.

Bang.

He hadn't done anything wrong—he wasn't humping Hawk like a fiend, wasn't mooning (much), and he wasn't being growly about his brothers cockblocking him at every turn all day.

But he wanted to.

He really wanted to scream at them that this was the first dragon he'd ever met who he wanted to bump uglies with, and they were cramping his style.

Badly.

Instead, he nibbled popcorn and stared at the big screen instead of looking at Hawk because he just didn't know what to do.

Are you well, sweet Rose?

No. He pouted. *I want to snuggle, and maybe ride you like a prize pony.*

Ah. Well, I would also like that, but I think I understand your brothers. They do not have your connection with me, so they do not know me as well as you already do. Hawk's red gold eyes wheeled at him.

Stupid. You're fine. This is boring.

Don't you dare tell him about the fact that we're a passageway now, Corbin warned. *What if he's a danger?*

He's not! Not Hawk. Hawk was good.

We don't know him.

Now he was back to wanting to punch. He knew Hawk was good. At least for them. And his brothers would expect him to believe them...

"I'm going to take a walk."

"Where?" Cullen asked, wide-eyed.

"Oh, you know. Around." Maybe he would go see the Rocky Mountain clutch. Or his mom.

"Outside?" Corbin growled, and he rumbled right back.

"Leave me be!" He stormed off, heading back into the house, letting his feet lead him.

My rose?

I'm just really grumpy!

All is well otherwise, though?

Yeah. I'm not stupid. I like you, you know? And his feelings were hurt.

I do. I like you as well. I would walk with you, but your brothers would just come. Hawk gave him a mental caress.

I'll be back. It's okay. I'm just going to see my friends.

And he turned left, pushing open the door into a wild blizzard, the blue flakes swirling madly, and he almost slammed the door behind him when he saw a bright red hood, eyes that sparkled with fury.

Shit.

"Cosmo?" That was Arielle's voice, Devon and Brand's daughter from the original Estes clutch. She was a teenager now, so fury was her default, but she'd surprised the fuck out of him.

"Hey, sweet pea! It's cold out here!" He went right to her. They had created a casita in the courtyard with an oven, because the dragons couldn't come into the house, not anymore. "Let's go into the casita and start the stove, huh?"

"Okay." She stomped along after him when she let him go. Wow, she was mad, huh? Kind of like him. They had called to each other.

They got the door open, then Arielle started the fire for them.

"Oh. Great job." He sat, inviting her to sit beside him. "You okay?"

"No. I'm really mad." She slumped down next to him, crossing her arms over her chest. Her cheeks were bright red under her freckles, and he thought it had nothing to do with the cold.

"I am too! Do you want to go first, or should I?"

"You go." Her green eyes glinted gold at him, and she tilted her head, clearly curious.

"Okay. I met someone, and my brothers are being asses about it."

"OMG! That's what's happening to me? I met a girl, and they won't let me go see her!"

"Oh, man." He didn't point out they were in a white-out blizzard. "What's she like?"

"She's amazing. She's a sea dragon, and she knows merpeople. Her best friend is a merman named Bubbles."

"His name is Bubbles?"

She grinned at him, blowing a little steam. "Not his real name. That's what he goes by. I'm going to go by Sparkle."

"Sparkle? That's pretty." Her fathers had to be losing their minds.

"Uh-huh."

"What's her name?"

"Siren."

"Oh, that's nice." And a little scary. "So, how did you meet?"

"There's a school. Like a traveling school. Sometimes, we meet up on the mountain, sometimes in town, sometimes on the beach." Arielle glowed, her eyes lit up. "I love it. I really do."

"That's great." Arielle had been pretty isolated most of her life, with just siblings and cousins to play with, so it was good to see her excited. "So why don't the folks want you to see her?"

"They say it's because of the snow, but you know they're lying! You know they are. They just don't like her."

"Hmm." No, he would bet it was far enough that they meant it. The snow meant no flying for kids.

"What about you?"

"Huh?"

She nudged him. "Why are your brothers being jerks?"

"Because they don't know this guy. I mean, I can hear him in my mind."

"O. M. G. Really? Like, you can really, really hear him?"

Cosmo nodded. "I can really, really hear him."

"Is it the same as you hearing your brothers?" Arielle was fascinated by mental communication. She was a bit of a hammer, in every psychic situation. And so it was very, very difficult for her to understand that someone was ever trying to speak to her.

He shook his head. "No, no, not the same. Not really at

all. I've always heard my brothers, you know, before I was born even. Hawk is new."

And that was the most fascinating part about it. Hawk was new. Hawk was *new* and wanted him without any thought.

Cosmo was used to having sex. He liked having sex. He'd had more than his fair share of sex, if he was honest.

But never with a dragon.

Never, ever with a full-blooded dragon.

Never ever, ever with a full-blooded ancient dragon that was hung like a...

Whoa. Stop.

Teenager.

"Dude, did you know that when you blush, you turn purple? NOT like Cullen's purple, but like *purple*." Arielle chuckled. "That kind of rocks."

"Yeah. I kind of feel like I'm blushing all the time right now. I just need the boys to understand how important he is because he really is important to me."

Arielle teared up, her eyes shimmering. "See, that's how I feel. I don't suppose you want to fly down with me and meet her?"

Cosmo shook his head. "Honey, I'm not a strong flyer at the best of times. I'm only half dragon, remember? I'm more flutter than power. This snow would knock me to the dirt."

She blinked, as if it had just occurred to her how dangerous it could be. "Well, I don't want you to get hurt."

"No, and I don't want you to get hurt." He winced and kind of shrugged a little bit. "I don't think your dads want you to get hurt either. I don't mean emotionally. I mean like, banging against the mountain hurt."

"Oh." She pondered that, and it was as if he could see

the wheels turning behind her eyes. "Well, why didn't they just say so?"

"Maybe they did, but you were just too mad?" He chuckled. "My dad is a big green dragon who can move the earth. When Corbin was a teenager, they fought about everything, and Mom would be like, why can't you talk? And Dad was like, I don't speak his language."

She burbled with laughter. "Yeah. Sometimes Poppy Brand and I just can't do it, and Da steps in. He's so much easier. Less alpha."

"That does make a difference." Alphas could be so damn stubborn.

"So you think they'll let me see her when the storm is over?"

"I bet they're eager to meet someone who captures your interest so much, and your pop is a great flier. He can take you down once it's safe."

"Okay, cool." She hugged him all of a sudden. "Thanks, Cosmo. I was so mad!"

"Oh, I hear you, kiddo. So was I." But he had a better perspective on it now.

Including the fact that he had left his brothers alone with Hawk, and they were either sitting in awkward silence or grilling him unmercifully. Yikes.

"Come on, kiddo. I might not fly you anywhere, but I will walk you back down to your house." He didn't want Brand and Devon frantic and out hunting for her in a storm in Lunastra. They still weren't used to the unpredictability of the weather in the dragonlands.

"Yeah? I bet Helena has made cookies!"

"Oh, that sounds good. How's Nevvy doing?"

"She's good. She and Sebby are best friends. Like *best* friends. It's so cute."

"I'm glad. She was so nervous about coming here."

"She's nervous about a lot, but Sebby is really sweet to her." She wrinkled her nose. "We're both firstborns. We kinda butt heads."

"Bang bang. Like goats."

"Oh, god, the goats." She laughed. "Sebby has those." She rolled her eyes. "I am not a farmer. Not. I am a *librarian.*"

"You are, huh? I know your dads are both book people."

"Uh-huh. So is Ollie. I love it. So I want to work at one of the big unis. Or in the village. Whatever."

"There are huge universities here?"

"Huge! There are big cities like Denver, but with dragons." She rolled her eyes. "Silly Cosmo."

"Wow. Do they look like human cities?" His dad was from the middle of nowhere, and there was a lot of Lunastra that he hadn't seen.

"No. No, they're wild. You'll have to see the books. Amazing! And—"

"Arielle! Arielle, where are you?" Tyson's roar filled the air.

"Uh-oh. They sent Uncle Ty."

"Whoops." Cosmo went to the door. "She's in here!" He waved furiously, hoping his pink showed through the blue. "Tyson! Here!"

"Is that you, Cosmo?" Tyson trudged up to the casita, peering at him through the snow and wind.

"It is. She's in here."

"Ah, good. Good. Ri, you scared us all to death."

"I—" She glanced at Cosmo, and he offered her a smile. "I'm sorry. I was mad. It was stupid."

Good girl.

Ty gave her an indulgent look as he stepped in to warm

his hands. "Well, reckless. You're never stupid. But your dads want to meet your friends. They just didn't want you to go right *now*."

"Yeah... Uncle Cosmo sort of told me that... I misunderstood and flew off the handle."

"Well, I think your dads will understand. Maybe we can apologize and make cookies?"

She nodded and went to Tyson for a hug. The huge dragon hugged her tight, then glanced at him.

"What are you doing out here? It's summer where you are."

"It is. My brothers made me mad." He winked at Arielle. "Now I need to go apologize."

"Is everything well?" Tyson asked, and he nodded.

"A new dragon is here. They're worried, and I'm—" Fascinated. "—intrigued."

"I see. Well, good luck, my friend."

Cosmo chuckled. "Thank you. I hope not to need it."

"I understand completely. I'm going to get Ri home. Are you well? Everything is well in the house?"

"Well..."

Ty stopped to stare at him. "What is it?"

"Myk's house. Did it have a tower room?"

"What? No. It started as a log home in the 50s, and then they added the fancy A-frame."

"So nothing remotely Victorian or neoclassical?"

"No."

"Then it is his house."

Tyson shook his head. "There's no tower room out here, Cosmo."

"There is out *there*, Tyson."

Ty stared at him. "No shit?"

"None detected."

"And who does it belong to supposedly?"

"An older alpha dragon named Hawk." That he was drawn to. That he wanted to touch. That he wanted to be touched by.

"Hmm." Tyson stroked his chin. Or rather, his beard. "Keep us informed."

"I will." As lore keepers if nothing else, they needed to ensure that this world kept decent records. It was important to all of them.

"Good night, Cosmo," Arielle said. "Come on, Uncle Ty. Cookies await."

"Good night, sweetheart. Stay safe. I'll come see you in a couple of days."

"Okay!" She dragged Ty out into the snow, and he waited for them to be well on their way before he banked the fire, putting it out as much as he needed to so he didn't have to worry about it burning down the casita.

Then he headed back to the house, ready to take on his brothers about where Hawk was going to sleep.

CHAPTER

FIVE

Obviously, the triplets didn't expect to have company.

Hawk stretched, trying to work out the crick in his neck from sleeping on the sofa. Admittedly, it was a nice long 1950s-style couch, but he was a large fellow, and his feet and head had hung at strange angles...

Cosmo had been sad that he wasn't allowed to go sleep in Cosmo's part of the house, he thought, but that was all right. That time would come soon enough, Hawk thought.

He rose early, as was his wont, and he wandered to the kitchen to investigate the food situation. There were some more modern foods he knew how to make. Bacon and biscuits. Flapjacks.

He found Cosmo leaning over the kitchen table, coffee mug in hand, pink hair all a mess. For a second, he couldn't breathe.

Was he hurt? Harmed? Dead? What?

About the time Hawk reached for him, Cosmo gave a long, slow snore.

Oh, bless him. Someone had been having trouble sleeping, he would bet.

"Cosmo…" He lifted Cosmo out of the chair and into his arms. "Come lie down on the couch."

"Mmm… Is there room for both of us?" Cosmo cuddled right in.

"There is." If he propped up pillows and sat rather than lying down… Which was worth it. "I was going to make breakfast."

"Mmhmm. In a minute. Now, just stay." Cosmo held him tight.

"I would like that." Like was such a pale word. He needed a phrase that spoke of the joy his body and soul felt when Cosmo touched him, smiled at him.

Cosmo cuddled under his chin, hands flattened over his heart. He grabbed a blanket, tugging it over them. Then he breathed in deep, taking in Cosmo's scent. "Hello, little rose."

"Mmm…hello, dragon. I couldn't sleep for needing you…"

"I know. I wanted you all night, and you seemed so far away in the tower." He kissed the top of Cosmo's head. "I am trying to respect your brothers, but it is difficult."

"Mmhmm. My bed is big. Really big." Cosmo sighed, wiggling against him.

"Is it?" He grinned, his body reacting to Cosmo's closeness and motion.

"Mmhmm, and I have lots of pillows and blankets."

"Shall we go to your room?" He rose again, lifting Cosmo. If Cosmo wasn't worried, then neither was he.

"Yes. Let's go. I need to be somewhere that's just us. Just the two of us, together." Cosmo licked him, nice and slow. "With a locked door."

He laughed, the sound husky to his own ears. "Absolutely. They shouldn't knock it down, should they?"

"No. No, they respect the boundaries more than that, I think." Cosmo did seem a bit worried, but he understood. This was a new situation.

He had a feeling Cosmo had done his share of going out and about and finding a partner for a night, but no one had ever invaded the brothers' space before.

And he was staying here with Cosmo and his house.

"I'm up at the top. I love the round room."

"That had been my room, sweet. Of course it's yours."

"Oh. I wonder where your bed is... I mean. I found mine in a storage room."

"Maybe it is mine, then. If it's as big as you say."

"It's like it was built for the space, you know?"

He trekked up to the round tower room, the one with the window he'd set by hand, and sure enough, that was his bed. He grinned, kissing Cosmo's cheek. "I do like your blankets and pillows."

"Thank you. I need to be cozy." Cosmo put his hands on his shirt, but didn't get farther than taking that off.

"I can see that." He watched. Cosmo had seen him fresh from his bath, but he hadn't seen all of Cosmo. And he wanted to. So bad that he was already hard and aching.

"I'm skinny," Cosmo admitted. "But I'm pretty."

"Oh, little rose. You're so perfect I can hardly bear it." He tugged off the sweater that almost fit him and the pants that were too short and too big in the waist. Corbin was stocky and shorter than he was.

Cosmo crawled into the bed, offering a long look at that perfect ass.

It made Hawk's mouth dry. He kicked free of the pants, then put one knee on the bed. "Be sure, Cosmo. If I come to bed with you, I will not just be sleeping." He wanted his Cosmo to see what he was getting. He was scarred, and his scales showed under his skin and on it, no matter how hard he tried to look human.

Cosmo surged over, bent, and sucked in the tip of his cock, not a hint of hesitation.

Oh, goddess. He arched up, his hips tilting. His ass clenched, his hand coming up to fist in Cosmo's hair. "Cosmo!" The sound that came out of him was a bit too loud, a bit shocked, as well. He thought nothing had ever felt this good.

Cosmo sucked him, and it occurred to him, that they'd never even kissed yet. Not touched fully, yet that mouth took his cock in, and Cosmo swallowed hard.

He wanted to just take what Cosmo offered, but he knew he also wanted to learn more about how Cosmo felt, how he tasted. So Hawk pulled him up, kissing his mouth like a starved creature.

Cosmo dug long fingers into his hair, holding them together as they feasted on one another. Cosmo tasted like...like a dessert from his childhood, which was so long ago. Honey and rosewater and a delicate earthiness that had to come from his fae side. So lovely.

"More," he growled when they broke for air, and he bit at Cosmo's lower lip.

"Definitely more," Cosmo murmured, cupping his cock, then stroking it up and down.

"Wicked rose."

"Yes. I love sex. I'm going to love sex with you even more." Cosmo was utterly unafraid, hands adoring his body.

"Yes, you are." He pushed a hand down Cosmo's back to lift him with his palm on Cosmo's ass.

Cosmo's happy laughter surprised him. "I do love a strong dragon."

"I am that," he admitted. Of all of the qualities that he knew he possessed for sure, he was unquestioningly confident in his strength.

Cosmo's eyes twinkled for him, the dark blue so surprising in the pale pink face. "You are. Now shut up and kiss me."

Oh, Hawk did adore a confident partner.

So he did as he was bidden, kissing Cosmo hard on the mouth, the taste of him exploding across Hawk's senses. He wanted more, and he had a feeling that sensation would never end. Not with Cosmo.

"Fuck, yes." Cosmo crawled up along his body, and they upended, crashing down onto the mattress. "Oops."

Hawk had twisted so he landed on the bottom, even if Cosmo wouldn't be harmed if he landed there. It came to him as instinct. Protect the omega.

Cosmo's eyes rolled, and so did the lean hips. "Oh, you feel just right..."

"So do you, sweet one." He stroked Cosmo's back, letting his hands wander where they would, testing the sweet, smooth skin and the scales he could feel pop up in places.

He'd never been intimate with a half-fae before, and the differences between them fascinated his fingers.

Every place that there would be hard ridges on his dragon form were rough in his human form, but not Cosmo.

Cosmo was leaner and longer, and he seemed to weigh only as much as a bird.

Hawk couldn't wait to see him in dragon form. Couldn't wait to see him fly.

He hummed, the noise almost a happy growl, and he could feel the air around them heat up from his breath.

"I need you to fuck me, dragon. I just want you to know that I need that."

"I will." His cock went from hard to molten hot hardened steel in moments. Just the words made his head spin.

"Thank you. My entire body is burning for you. Buzzing for you."

"I can feel it. You're very smooth and lovely, little rose. I want to taste all of you."

Cosmo stretched up, tall and then even taller. "I can be yours."

The words buzzed through the air and locked in the base of his brain.

"Oh, be very careful what you offer, little changeling." He could just eat Cosmo up, then take him to his hoard, should he ever find it again, and keep him there forever.

"I may be little, but we've been around for a long time." Cosmo shot him a wicked, knowing grin. "There is absolutely nothing in me that's a child. I know exactly what I'm offering."

Hawk's mouth went absolutely dry.

It took him a moment to remember how to breathe, but once he did, he decided to take Cosmo's offer for all it was worth. "I accept."

Then he surged up to smash their lips together in a fierce, no-holds-barred kiss.

Cosmo met him with an equal fervor, and Hawk swore the entire room turned red and began to glow as if lava had covered the floor and was dripping from the walls themselves.

His grip on Cosmo's ass tightened, and he melded them

together, his cock rising hard and needy, his knot making itself known.

"Uhn." Cosmo devoured him, not letting up one second in intensity. In fact, he got a little toothy, a little thorny, his sweet rose. Cosmo gave as good as he got, and Hawk loved that.

He could become addicted to it.

Turning Cosmo beneath him, Hawk began stripping off Cosmo's clothing, needing all of that sweet skin to be bare.

It took forever and yet no time at all for them to be bare to one another's hands and eyes.

"Fuck, I want you," Cosmo moaned, and the heat in those blue eyes honored Hawk, made him hard and caused his balls to draw up.

"You have me."

"I want all of you." Cosmo's tongue slid along his jaw toward his ear, and he was shuddering by the time Cosmo whispered, "I need your knot. I want to feel you for days."

"I will give you everything you desire." He would feel Cosmo surrounding him, and he would make it good for his new love.

He spread Cosmo beneath him, exploring all of his textures and scents and flavors. Hawk couldn't get enough, and he panted, licking Cosmo's belly on the way to taste that hard cock that curved up toward his mouth.

"Yes!" Cosmo arched, bucking toward his lips as soon as they encircled the tip of his cock.

He sucked Cosmo in deep, licking the head as he pulled back. Hawk wasn't afraid to do this; in fact, he loved it. He knew where the real power lay when he was with a lover, and it was in giving pleasure, not taking it.

Cosmo's face was a study in absolute utter bliss.

He had seen many lovers over the centuries like this. But now it was different.

Cosmo's eyes were not closed.

Indeed, they stared at him, watching every second, taking everything in. As if he was quenching a deep thirst.

One long-fingered hand reached down, sliding through his hair for only a moment before coming to cup his jaw.

Those fingers curled towards his chin, thumb gently massaging his temple.

"I saw you," Cosmo whispered. "I didn't know it was you then, but I do now. I saw you."

He looked up, releasing Cosmo from his mouth to slide up and take a kiss. *Yes. In your dreams. Your visions.*

And he had seen Cosmo looking for him, had known it was not just his house and his hoard he was searching for. It had been Cosmo who had called to him, drawing him there to find what he truly desired.

He pushed one hand down under Cosmo to press a finger against Cosmo's hole, testing his readiness.

Wet and slick, his omega—his—was eager and ready for his prick.

Cosmo grabbed his own knees and pulled himself wide open, exposing himself fully, without a single hint of shame. Filled with desire. "Don't stop."

"I won't." His own prick was heavy between his thighs, aching to be buried in that place that it was intended for, that he was made for.

He muscled up in between Cosmo's legs and lifted Cosmo's ass as his fingers slipped free. He guided the tip of his cock into Cosmo's ready hole.

Hawk worried for a moment that he was too large, that perhaps his dragon wouldn't fit inside this perfect mate.

Cosmo didn't seem to have the same worry, because he

surged up and pushed down, taking him into the root without a single hesitation.

Both of them gasped at the sudden motion, Cosmo throwing his head back and arching his throat.

Hawk stilled, worried until he heard Cosmo moan.

"Fuck yeah."

"So perfect." He felt steam rise up around them. "Cosmo."

Cosmo grinned wildly, baring his teeth. "You said my name. Not Rosie or changeling. My name."

"Your beautiful name. Never think I don't know it." He bit at Cosmo's throat, just hard enough to sting but not bruise.

"More," Cosmo gasped, hand on the back of his head, keeping him right where he was.

"More," Hawk agreed, moving his hips, pressing down into Cosmo's body.

Hawk could feel the magic swirling around them, seeming to grow tighter, like Cosmo's body around his prick.

The world became smaller and smaller and smaller, closing in to just this amazing bed that was theirs.

It had been his, been Cosmo's, but now it was theirs, and they were creating—

Something inside him stopped, and he heard the tiniest whisper.

Life.

So he stilled, eyes on Cosmo, willing his lover to focus on him.

"What is it? What's the matter?"

"Do you feel that?" He searched Cosmo's eyes, hoping for some recognition. "It's new."

"Yes." Cosmo panted softly, hands sliding down his arms. "It wants to be new, a life... Is it the wrong time?"

He loved that it was not "the wrong thing" or "the wrong idea," but the wrong time.

"No, love. It is the perfect time. You are—This is something I have never done in all my long life." His knot swelled as if to emphasize what he was saying. This was beyond anything he'd ever experienced.

This was mating.

"Then it's the right time. Now, focus. We're very, very busy, hmm?" Cosmo's laughter filled him with pure joy.

"We are indeed." He was through wondering and thinking. Cosmo was right there, hot and willing and so wet it made Hawk's eyes cross. All he had to do was start moving again, because the friction felt like flying too high and then reentering the atmosphere. Like diving into a volcano.

Like crossing the veil when he was wide-awake.

This is real. Cosmo's thought was as clear and as sharp as an arrow to the chest. *This is real.*

Hawk wasn't sure exactly why Cosmo would think it wasn't, so he nodded, sweat rolling down his face as his hips worked. *Real. Yes.*

Really, that was the best he could do, right now.

A single tear rolled down Cosmo's cheek, and if he had felt for a moment any hint of sorrow in the bond that was quickly forming between them, he would have stopped, but all he felt was this overwhelming, incredible joy.

It pushed through his chest, down deep into his gut, and ran up his spine to explode in his brain. He felt so much love already, and he barely knew anything about this wondrous fae dragon. He could only imagine what he would feel in a few years. Decades. Longer.

"Focus, dragon." Cosmo laughed for him again, but this

time, the sound was broken, husky, proving to Hawk how much Cosmo was affected by their lovemaking.

"I'll show you focus." Hawk went for a smile, knowing without question that it was more feral than anything. His dragon was so close to the forefront that it was almost tangible. The room was heating up, his scales were popping out, and the whole world smelled of roses.

The scent made him dizzy, and he breathed it in deeply. He thrust faster, his body on fire, his nerves firing rapidly. He could feel how Cosmo softened around him, then tightened, allowing him to push deeper and deeper inside, right to where his knot needed to seat. Needed to lodge.

Cosmo stopped teasing, stopped laughing, stopped doing anything that wasn't focused on them and their pleasure. The pink body suffused with a darker rose, the beautiful skin almost glowing.

In this moment, Cosmo looked more fae than dragon, the lean features angular and hard with his need.

Hawk could feel it when Cosmo got close. His balls drew up, and his body tightened impossibly.

He grunted, his hips moving in tiny pops, his knot held deep and hard inside Cosmo. Hawk pushed a hand down between them, grabbing Cosmo's cock to try to send him over the edge.

They needed to have this little death.

Cosmo roared when he came, his own personal fountain of lava pouring over Hawk's hand.

That was all he needed, just that shove to come himself. To fill Cosmo's body with his seed. He gritted his teeth, the scent of brimstone rising around them as he shot, his knot swelling more than he could even imagine.

So tight. Impossibly so.

His chest heaved, and when he collapsed, he rolled sideways, taking Cosmo with him so he didn't crush him.

The magic seemed to coalesce around them. To lock them together, to lock them down on this bed, and he'd never felt anything like it.

He wasn't sure that it was possible to feel anything like this with anyone other than this particular being. And he was ecstatic about it.

Hawk couldn't stop smiling. In fact, his cheeks literally hurt from it, the muscles so unused to flexing that way. He'd been asleep so long.

"Beautiful dragon." Cosmo smiled at him, eyelids heavy. "Cover us up. Let's snuggle. It's early."

"What about breakfast?" he teased.

Cosmo waved one hand, the motion lazy and loose. "Someone will cook it. If they don't, we'll brave the snow and go over to Tyson's. Let's see if Helena will feed us. She's amazing."

"I have no idea who those people are, but I am willing." He would follow Cosmo anywhere. Hellfire didn't faze him.

They are friends. On the other side of the veil, Cosmo tilted his head, blinked at him. *Do you know about the veil?*

"I do..." He hesitated a minute. "Is the veil still open?"

"Is this a trick question? I'm way too into the afterglow to answer trick questions right now."

Hawk frowned again, but it was all fine. Cosmo was right. Whatever was going to happen wouldn't change between now and a couple of hours from now and breakfast.

Then he would discover what Cosmo meant, because if the veil was still open, then he could go back to Lunastra.

SIX

The knock made Cosmo stir, and he found he could move away from Hawk. They slid apart, and he grabbed his robe on the way to the door. Whoa. He was a little sore and a lot...bowlegged.

He cracked the door open. "What?"

"Breakfast. Come on. We're going to Ty's." One of Corbin's green eyes peered at him through the tiny opening he'd made.

"See? I told Hawk that was what we would do."

"You fucked him."

"First, fucked is just not a very nice word." Cosmo stopped, chuckled, then rolled his eyes. "God, yes. Do you blame me? He's beautiful."

"I kind of blame you." Corbin sighed and shook his head. "Still, it doesn't matter. We're going to go to breakfast, and—" Corbin stopped. "What if he can't go through?"

"What?"

What did that even mean? Of course. Hawk could go through. Hawk was a dragon.

"Well, the other dragons can't come through this way. We can meet them out there, but they can't get through…"

"Oh." Cosmo hadn't considered that. "Fuck that's bad."

Not that Hawk couldn't go out, but if Hawk went out, then Hawk couldn't come back in. And if Hawk couldn't go out and come in, then Hawk couldn't be in his house, which was where Cosmo lived.

And Cosmo wasn't living out there because his brothers lived in here and their whole, entire job was to guard this house.

Oh, this was a problem.

Was it fair to just not to talk about the veil with Hawk at all? To not show him where to go.

Seemed like the easiest answer.

"Well, I don't like this at all," Cosmo told his brother. "We have to fix this."

Corbin's lips twisted. "But if we fix it, then we open the veil again, and then dragons can come in and out at will, and I don't think that's the way this is supposed to work."

"We don't know how the hell anything's supposed to work. We are just making this up as we go along, and we both know it. All three of us know it." He was not going to scream. Not.

"True. But we have to at least pretend that we understand this, otherwise people won't trust us when we let them come, and you know, tell them they have to go in. Everyone says that the dragons will come here to get into the veil." Corbin always had an answer for everything.

Cosmo wasn't sure what to even say about all this because there was also an opening to the Land of Summer, and he was pretty sure that the dragons weren't supposed to go in there, even though Dad was in there. This was hurting his head. "How come nobody just lets you have sex and sleep anymore?"

"Do you want me to just bring you bacon?"

"Yeah. Can you just bring me, like, a lot of bacon? Possibly some pastries or something? I'm really hungry, and if I'm really hungry, then he's got to be super hungry."

"Of course. You know that I won't let you starve. Much. And then, only when I'm mad at you." Corbin stared into the bedroom again, then he got an evil grin. "Was it good?"

"Absolutely fucking stunning. I mean. Like whoa."

Corbin groaned. "Really?"

"Uh-huh. Tell me what I want to hear." He waggled his eyebrows at his brother.

"I am so jealous."

He threw the door open and hugged his brother hard. Partially because he loved his weird, crazy elder brother, but mostly because it was really fun to hear Corbin squeal about bodily fluids because...naked!

Cullen would have been even more horrified, but he would take this.

Once his brother left, he went back to sit next to Hawk on the bed, hand on Hawk's warm belly. He was like a furnace.

"What's wrong, sweet?"

"It's obvious, huh?"

"A little bit, yes." Hawk sat up, dragging Cosmo into his lap. "Talk to me."

"So...the veil opened, and a bunch of dragons went in, most of them." That was the easy part.

"Yes, I assumed that was what happened. I missed it, I realize." Hawk gave him a wry sort of smile.

"Yeah. Yeah, you did. Anyway, that was where I wanted

to go for breakfast. But dragons who cross the veil don't seem to be able to come back."

"Ah. You are worried I would be stuck."

"Yes, I just found you. I don't want you to go off into this big, huge, magical, wonderful dragon space and not be coming back, especially not when I have to be here to be like Super Guardian Man. And let me tell you how unfair it is that I have to be all Super Guardian Man with my brothers when we're not very big. I don't know if you've noticed. I mean, we're very, very smart and we're kind of mean and we're super good at really screwing things up and making people miserable. But like. Guardians, no."

He just thought Hawk should know.

Hawk blinked at him, kind of frowned a little bit, leaned in. "I have no wish to leave you."

"Well, that's nice." And it was comforting, although it didn't actually answer any questions, because how long could anyone be happy just staying in this one house? I mean, he could go toodling over to the Land of Summer and see his mum; he could go out and see Arielle. He could go out into the human world, even though everyone thought that he was a little strange and possibly permanently flushed. If he had a dime for every human person that had asked if he had rosacea, he would have a lot of dimes.

"So what does that mean in practicality? Because you and I both know that no one can just stay in a house."

"I do not know." Hawk spread his hands. "I mean, I woke up in a cave recently. And…" Those dark cheeks flushed even darker. "I am sure your brothers would not be pleased to hear that some say I am not stable, my love. I have slept a great deal since the dawn of the new century."

He frowned. "Like since the early 2000s?"

"Oh, have we changed, then?"

"Oh yeah that was a while ago. Not too terribly long, but a while."

Regardless, that didn't answer the question about what they were going to do if Hawk went over to Lunastra and then couldn't come back.

Cosmo didn't want to live in a casita. He wasn't one hundred percent sure that he wanted to live where it was winter in June. Just like he didn't know if he wanted to live where it was summer all the time.

But he did know that he wanted to live with his brothers. They'd always been together, and he wasn't ready to discuss them not being that way.

"At any rate, I told them to bring breakfast back. We at least have to discuss this."

Although maybe they didn't have to discuss it. It wasn't like Hawk was officially his, or even unofficially his. It was sort of like not a thing.

People and dragons and fae, they did what they needed to do, and just because Cosmo wanted him to stay, didn't mean Hawk wanted to stay.

Goddess, his head hurt.

"We are officially ours." Hawk touched his cheek. "At least that is how I feel. But if you find you cannot reconcile me with your life, my little rose, I understand." Hawk's expression shut down some. "I am difficult."

"You are?"

"Yes." Hawk didn't elaborate, but he could tell this was going to be a thorny subject.

"Why? I mean, is it a choice? Because we could all just be easy for a while."

Hawk's laugh was like a rusty gate swinging. "I will try for you, but Cosmo, I am old. I have forgotten many things. I hurt sometimes. I was born in Lunastra and I was thrust out and I never could get back. I think it tore something in me."

Oh.

Cosmo stopped suddenly and looked at Hawk, horrified. "Hurting? Oh, dear. Well, then no. No. If you need to go. Then you have to go."

He wouldn't have Hawk hurting, not for something as silly as just being with him. Not when Cosmo could go out and come back and do whatever he needed to. That was... Well, it was mean.

And he wasn't mean.

He never thought he was mean.

Do you want to go now? Cosmo had no idea what was going to happen, but he'd spent an enormous amount of time with the universe telling him what was going to happen and him not understanding what that meant.

This wasn't much different.

"Do we need to find your hoard first? Or if I find it, do you want me to bring it to you? I don't even know what I'm looking for and I sure haven't found it yet. But I've been busy."

Hawk stroked his back, hands never still. "Not if you cannot come with me. Not if I cannot be here, in your home with you. There's a reason you are between worlds. A purpose. I can feel it." Hawk took one of his hands and put it over Hawk's heart. "Here."

"Yes, but—"

"Mmm. No buts. I feel certain I would not truly belong there anymore, either. It has been...millennia."

"Oh, so you've been gone a long time."

Hawk blinked at him, obviously confused. "Yes. You don't seem to be confused by that."

Cosmo snorted. Confused? Him? "Why would I? My

people have been around for millennia." Cosmo imagined he was old enough to have seen civilizations rise and fall. What was time to him?

Sometimes, he thought entire worlds came and went in the moments that he was just playing ball or chasing his brothers through the grass.

In the Land of Summer, time meant very little.

Not to people like him.

Hawk chuckled. "You are different, aren't you? Unique in all the world."

"Not at all. There are two carbon copies of me, a green one and a lavender one."

"No. No, they are lovely and bright, and they keep things growing and sow illusions... But you shine like a beacon. You are a perfect rose in a thorny land, my love." Hawk waxed poetic for him, and it made his heart melt. Goddess, Hawk was like no one he'd ever met in his whole life.

He wasn't sure he could just let Hawk walk away into the dragonlands.

"We'll figure it out."

That was Cosmo's position—they had plenty of time. What else were they going to do?

They could explore the house.

Make love.

Obviously, Hawk could go outside into the human world, so it wasn't like he was being confined to a house.

Oh...house arrest. How funny was that? Cosmo started laughing, the giggles just kind of pouring out of him, and Hawk looked at him as if he had lost his mind.

Which maybe he had. He was considering house arrest of the biggest dragon he'd ever seen.

"What's so funny, my rose?"

"It's hard to explain. It's going to take hours and hours of CSI to get you to get this."

"CSI?"

Oh dear... "How do you feel about television?"

He knew how he felt about television—which was the boob tube was a fabulous thing, and there was a reason that he had agreed to become the guardian of the veil.

He not only got cable; he got Amazon deliveries on a regular basis, because goddess knew those at the Estes clan had requests.

Daily.

He was going to buy stock in Doritos.

CHAPTER
SEVEN

Hawk wandered in Cosmo's part of the house.

They'd had breakfast. TV and snacks. He liked Funyuns. They tasted like onions, but dry and strange.

He also liked the sweet and salty nuts. Where he'd lived, there had been hazelnuts. So fresh.

When he'd told Cosmo that, Cosmo had made him a coffee with hazelnut-flavored syrup...

But now Cosmo was with his brothers, who had insisted on some sort of family meeting. So he started in the tower, just seeing what parts of his house had carried over.

The tower room was obviously, where Cosmo had spent most of his time, and in the restroom, which had been... modernized and made glorious.

Bathing with a lover was proving to be stunning.

The walls were draped with silken scarves woven with patterns of every color of pink and red and blue that he could imagine.

There were dozens and dozens of tiny strings with crystals in them to sparkle when the light hit. The bed was his, of course, and he remembered it fondly.

But the blankets and the pillows and the curtains? Those were all his Rose.

Someone liked his creature comforts.

He stared at the big wardrobe that was in the corner. He remembered that as well. The wardrobe held clothes.

He stared at it.

That wardrobe held clothes. His clothes. He needed comfortable clothes.

He stared, and he could feel lava bubbling up inside of his belly.

The magic waited, right there.

"I need clothes," he whispered, and the wardrobe seemed to tremble in the space where it was sitting.

"I need clothes," he said, just a little louder.

He could feel the magic in this place waking up. Or maybe it was him that was waking up. It didn't matter. He could feel it rumbling from deep within the mountain, and all he had to do was reach for it.

"I need clothes," he roared, the house shaking, and the wardrobe door popped open. Spilling dozens and dozens of sweaters and T-shirts and soft, comfortable pants and hats and scarves.

And boots and slippers—oh, he'd loved slippers—came pouring out.

That was better.

Cosmo came running in. "What the hell was that?"

Cosmo caught sight of the clothing and gasped. "Look what you did!"

There was something glorious about the utter joy his rose took in everything.

No amount of magic frightened him.

It was as if the universe had offered him someone who simply accepted the oddness that was him.

"I needed clothes," he explained. "This seemed easier than asking a warrior princess to deliver them."

Cosmo blinked at him, tilted his head. "Obviously. Yes. Shall we sort through them? You do like red and black, don't you? I think it suits you." Cosmo brought him a bright red sweater that was so warm and squishy that he wanted to touch it for hours. "It's probably too warm to wear this right now, but excellent choice."

"I can wear it. I'm warm all the time anyway." He pulled off the borrowed shirt he wore and slipped on the sweater. He might just pet it all day. "Now pants? And a pair of slippers, please. You choose."

Cosmo laughed so easily. "Of course. Hmm. There are these black pants. Look at them. So sweet. And here are socks and the perfect slippers for exploring."

Oh, yes. He took what he was offered, wallowing a little in Cosmo's care.

"Would you like me to brush your hair?" Cosmo asked, so casual.

Hawk thought he might die. Simply expire. Just slump to the bed like a fairy-tale princess in a deep sleep.

Or explode with utter joy. Poof and he would be gone.

"Would you mind?"

He wore his ebony hair in long braids because, while he did keep it clean, brushing it was just an enormous hassle.

The thought of Cosmo caring enough to tend to him in this way? Made Hawk a little dizzy.

"Of course I wouldn't mind. Let me go get the oil and the brush." Cosmo scampered off like he was eager to do this chore.

Hawk sat on the bed, legs crossed as he waited almost breathlessly for his lover to come back out.

When he did, Cosmo brought a huge round wooden hairbrush with fine bristles, along with a comb and a tiny crystalline bottle of oil. "We use this on our hair. It keeps it supple. Yours obviously needs some love, but it's a beautiful color. I always wanted black hair. I dyed mine once, you know. It was a disaster, trust me. Black and pink—not a natural combination. It was kind of great, but not natural."

He couldn't imagine. Cosmo's hair was perfect as it was. "Where do you want me?"

"You can just sit right there, wherever you're comfortable. I'll kneel behind you."

He stayed where he was, and Cosmo climbed up on the bed behind him, settling in to remove one of the dozens of braids that he had controlling his wild mane.

"This is going to be fun."

Hawk chuckled softly. "No, this is going to be arousing."

"Oh, naughty dragon." Cosmo petted him, hands on his back, his hair. He hummed. It was just the best feeling, having Cosmo care for him. He loved the feel of Cosmo's fingers sorting out all the strands of his hair.

"I can be naughty, I suppose." But this wasn't so much about that.

"There's a time and a place for naughty," Cosmo agreed. "But this is more basic, more necessary, I think." Cosmo hummed as he worked, fingers incredibly gentle. "You did a lovely job creating your clothes."

"Thank you." Hawk thought so too. It was satisfying to know that the magic had responded so easily. He was a touch rusty.

Possibly quite a bit rusty.

"It's been a long time since I had to use it—the magic—and when I woke up, it felt as if it was very far away."

"Well, your heart was all the way across the country. I mean, I'm assuming it's here, since your magic is working."

Hawk nodded, because he had no doubt. "It's here."

He wasn't sure exactly where, but then again, he really hadn't done more than stay up here in the tower room.

Naked.

In bed.

Perhaps it would be wise at some point to go down and speak to Cosmo's brothers again and explain himself.

Let them know that while he was not in any way stealing their brother, he also intended not to go anywhere without him. Even if that meant just staying in here.

He thought they might let him use other parts of the house, however. They were reasonable types, if worried about their brother. He smiled. How could he blame them? It wasn't every day that an old dragon such as himself showed—

"Ow."

"Sorry, love." Cosmo kissed his head. "Bad tangle there, but I got it. What are you thinking about so hard?"

Hawk shrugged. "About going downstairs."

"Oh." Cosmo slowly worked out another tangle. "That seems reasonable. We could all have supper together, especially now that you have clothes. It's important to have your own things so that you feel comfortable."

Hawk didn't point out that most of the things in this house *were* his things. Not all of them, of course.

Some of them were Cosmo's, some of them were just totally unfamiliar to both of them.

He assumed that meant they belonged to the poor dragons who had been killed.

"I don't think so, love." Cosmo shook his head. "I'm not sure that this house was here when Myk lived here. I'm pretty sure that that's the part of the house that Corbin's in."

"So...how many houses are here?" And why? Hawk couldn't figure out why on earth, when there was actually space to be had, that his home would become amalgamated with another.

"We think three, but it could possibly be four." Cosmo started on another braid. "It could be as much as five, if you count the fact that Myk's family possibly had three that were one."

"What?" Hawk wasn't following.

"Okay, so there were three dragons—Myk and his brothers, and they had mates. Not Myk, but the brothers. Then there were babies—again, not Myk, but the brothers. And they each had a place in the house that was theirs, and I don't know if it was just one house or if it was three houses made one." Cosmo took a deep, deep breath. "Because I do know that Myk moved to Tyson's house, which was actually one house, but it kept growing, and now it's basically three separate houses plus this amazing place for children at the bottom."

"And this is on the other side of the veil?"

Cosmo kissed the top of his head again. "Yes."

"And did it start that way?" he asked, trying to get a handle on this.

"No. It started in Estes, in the mountain, and then it kind of mooched across the veil."

"The house."

"And the mountain, I think."

Hawk was developing a headache. "All right. Back to the

original question. This house. It was just mine. It was in California."

"Right. Except that this is not California. This is Colorado, and this is in the mountains."

Hawk might have to kill him. "Yes, love, but…" Hawk took a deep breath. Let it out. "So, this house. Did it look like this when Myk and the brothers had it?"

"Oh excellent question! Good job! I know this one." Cosmo waved his hand, and the brush went flying. It had a little bit of his hair with it and that hurt. He was kind of stunned, but he didn't say anything because Cosmo was having a moment, and Hawk didn't want to interrupt him. "So if you look at this house from the other side, it looks just like Myk's house, but if you look at this house from this side… Like if you go outside here and look up, then there's the tower room. There's no tower room on the other side!"

"Hmm. Well, that's interesting."

"I thought so. I mean, it keeps changing. But not on the side that Myk can see. Maybe it would hurt him for it to be all different."

"The brush, love."

"Oh, whoops." Cosmo retrieved it. "Anyway, I think we each got a little of the house that we wanted, if you get me."

"So you wanted my house?" He was trying to wrap his mind around it. Perhaps something in him had called to Cosmo, and Cosmo had finally heard it.

Cosmo got quiet, and Hawk turned to look at him. "What's wrong?"

"It's nothing, I mean. It is something but…" Cosmo sighed. "I mean, you're going to figure it out eventually, I'm sure. But I wanted… I wanted a part of the house that…that wasn't sad all the time. It didn't have all the blood and the bad memories from before. The vampires did terrible things. I can't even go in the basement."

"But it's over now," he pointed out, and Cosmo shrugged, obviously embarrassed.

"That doesn't matter. I have problems with that sort of thing. I see things, you know, and sometimes, if there's too much, I just... It gets ugly."

"A seer, of course. That makes a lot of sense," he told Cosmo. "I totally understand what you're saying. The echoes of all of that must be incredibly loud."

"So you're not freaked out?" Cosmo asked.

"Why should I be? Having a seer around is not the strangest thing I have seen in the last millennia."

He received an icy look. "Right. You must have seen lots of things that make me seem just...average. Normal."

And now he'd hurt Cosmo's feelings. He gathered his lover in close to try to rectify that. "Of course you're not normal or average. You're mine, and you're amazing. I'm not worried about you being a seer. We all have our talents."

"I just wish mine was cooler. The boys both have neat ones. Mine is relatively pointless. It shows me things that happened. It shows me things that might happen, but it's not particularly useful. Like, I don't know when something bad is going to happen, or even if it is bad because I've had a vision of you, and it was scary because I didn't know who you were. I just knew that it wasn't as if my brain said 'oh look, your mate is coming, and it's going to be amazing'. No, it was all like 'boo, big scary dragon. Everybody run! Fire, fire!' See it's useless."

"It's not useless. Such magic never is." He shook his head firmly. "You are amazing. And the gift of sight is often clouded with difficulty. I suppose it's a give and take..." He pondered that, then shrugged. "But here I am, and not a 'boo' in sight."

Cosmo nodded. "No. No, you're not a boo. You're a…"

He got a long, lazy glance, and Cosmo licked his lips.

"Mmmhmm. We're supposed to dine with your brothers, which we will not manage if you continue to look at me that way." He did enjoy how Cosmo liked sex.

How could he not? Hawk loved sex with Cosmo too.

"Yeah. No fair. Still, I think you need to meet the brothers on a more equal level. They're going to like you." Cosmo didn't sound particularly worried, which was handy.

Not that it mattered. Cosmo was his, and he wasn't going anywhere, and so the other two had no choice but to learn to deal with him.

Just as he had no choice but to learn to deal with them. It was a give and take situation.

"Are the clothes that I have on suitable for dinner with your family?"

"Whatever clothes make you feel happy and comfortable are appropriate clothes. We're not fancy. Trust me." Cosmo ran the brush through his hair, and Hawk's eyes crossed. "Now my mother, she's fancy."

"Oh?" Hawk was fascinated to hear. He had met a few fae in his life, but he'd never gotten to know any personally.

"Yes, flowers are her talent, and so her home is a bower, and every meal is blossoms and tea cakes. Every so often you just want to dig into a huge steak and tear it apart with your teeth."

Why did that sound so sexual?

"Does she not partake of meat?"

"Only when she's grumpy." Cosmo began to braid his hair into a single, long tail. "Dad, however, he's kind of a carnivore. He tends to wander out when he needs something amazing. He gorges on brisket and steak and burgers and chicken until he's full. Then he'll wander back home, take a two-month-long nap, and then wake up renewed for quite a while."

Parents. How interesting to have a mate with parents. Especially ones that he could possibly see, interact with. He assumed that some of his former lovers had had parents. It just had never come up. He wasn't sure that he had parents, and if he did, they were probably sound asleep at this point.

So he would just meet Cosmo's family and assimilate into them. He hoped.

"There we go." Cosmo patted his braid. "All set."

"Thank you, love."

"You're welcome. We'll take a shower tonight and I'll wash it for you. I love the color."

"Oh, yes, please. Is there anywhere to swim nearby?"

"There are rivers, but they're cold. My brother says that there are natural heated springs down inside the mountain though. He says he can smell them, so this winter, we're going to go find them."

"Oh, so you're going spelunking then?" That actually sounded like fun. He could help with that.

"I guess we are. I just think the idea of having somewhere safe to float—safe enough for four dragons to float? It's important. We just have to hunt it. That's not my gift."

"You're not a dowser, are you?"

"I don't think so. Seems like it would very much be Corbin's job. Not mine."

"Hmm." He thought about that. If it was a natural spring, heated by geothermal energy, he ought to be able to find it. Hawk had a real feeling for that kind of thing buried deep in the earth. He was drawn to magma...

Could be because he could spit lava, but who knew? Hawk didn't question such things as the talent given to each dragon. Eventually it would end up being just what they needed it to be.

Cosmo sighed, pecking a kiss on the back of his neck before climbing off the bed. "We ought to go make nice."

"I'm ready. This is going to be fun." Hawk had made up his mind. He was not going to fight with Cosmo's brothers.

He was going to become family.

Dammit.

EIGHT

"So what's for dinner?" Cosmo was going for cheery and bouncy, and he was not going to have a meltdown.

Not tonight.

Not again.

They'd already come to blows about Hawk and sex and leaving the house and heading into the veil and whether or not they should take Hawk out to Lunastra and all sorts of things that were none of their business.

But that didn't matter. Not tonight.

Tonight, they were just going to be gently social.

"Roast and potatoes."

It was obvious that they'd been over in the dragon veil side of the world because it was still snowing and bitter over there, and it didn't matter that it was like summer here and they should be having corn and tomatoes.

"Sounds perfect," Hawk said. "Is there anything I can do?"

Don't do it, he warned Corbin and Cullen.

What? We're nice. They both went wide-eyed, and then they shook their head in unison. "We're good. Have a seat."

"Thanks for offering," Cosmo told Hawk, and then went over to peer at the Yorkshire puddings in the oven and at the roast. It all smelled just fine.

Not poisoned.

All in all, it seemed like it was going to be just fine.

"Did the guys send their mail-in orders?" He was in charge of internet requests, and he would make an order this week.

"Orders?" Hawk asked.

Cosmo nodded and rubbed his hands together. "We are the provider of all things naughty. Doritos. Cheetos. Chips. Chocolate. Chewing gum." He counted all of the snacks off on his fingers. "Oh Combos. Pringles. Sour cherry balls. Oreos. Hostess Cupcakes." Cullen cracked up this time. "They all want different kinds of hot chocolate, and Pop Rocks."

Cosmo tilted his head. "Why do they want Pop Rocks in their hot chocolate? It's not like you could see it."

Corbin threw his hands wide and expansively. "Who knows the ways of dragons?" Then he shot Hawk a wicked grin. "I mean, they are mysterious, aren't they?"

"Some would say so, yes." Hawk smiled back, serene as a duck gliding along on top of a lake. He figured that had to be maddening for his brothers. Nothing seemed to ruffle Hawk. And honestly, if Hawk was old or as crazy as he said he was, then why should he get upset about a couple of upstart fae dragons?

That boggled his mind if he thought about it too much.

"Also, Sebby would like whatever the new Mario game is." Sebby, who was the oldest of the huge crop of kids from the Utah clutch, had a Nintendo Switch, and he managed somehow to keep it charged, but he couldn't get new games but through them.

"Don't his dads worry? I mean about them somehow making the games come to life or something?" Cullen always worried. "I think I'd be careful about that sort of thing."

Cosmo blinked over. "That couldn't happen."

"It might; you don't know." Well, Cullen did have a point.

That would be kind of cool though.

Corbin frowned. "You don't think..."

They all three looked at Hawk, because honestly, this could become a huge problem on a lot of different levels.

Hawk blinked at them. "What?"

Cosmo started. "So video games..."

"Will the magic make them come alive?"

"Is this something that the kids could do?"

"Because if this is something they could do, that would be bad."

"People eating mushrooms."

"Stars that make gold bars fall out of the sky."

"And then there's those weird gorilla things and that ghost thing with the hat."

"This is just bad."

"Are we perpetuating badness?"

"People don't eat mushrooms anymore?" Hawk looked at them like they'd lost their minds. "I think someone's going to have to explain."

"Which part?" Cosmo asked, even as Cullen blurted out,

"I mean, what are we going to do if all of a sudden there's a market that shows up that's being run by bears?"

"I'd be more concerned about the cars, guys. Sebby and Arielle racing each other with cars that can shoot things at each other. This is the problem." Corbin's eyes were big as saucers.

Hawk held up his hands. "You're all very confusing. And... Don't talk. One at a time. Cosmo, you start. I do know what cars are."

"Oh fuck." Cosmo stared at his brothers. He didn't even know how to process someone whose life experience ended with "I know what cars are". "Maybe we should start with supper."

Corbin nodded. "That's smart. Let's start with supper. Then I think we're going to have to have show-and-tell."

Cullen tilted his head. "Do they have a last hundred-year wrap-up thing on the History Channel?"

"Do we get the History Channel?" Cosmo wasn't sure...

"We can get a free two-week subscription. Surely he can learn everything he needs to know in that time."

Cosmo thought Corbin had a great idea. However, he was going to hold off on getting anybody the last anything game until they figured this whole thing out, because surely this was sort of like introducing scary frogs to Australia.

Or possibly like introducing dragons into the Land of Summer.

It seemed like a good idea at the time, but it caused so many problems.

Cullen shook his head. "Roast and potatoes and I made Yorkshire puddings."

"Yum." Cosmo winked at Hawk. "Do you know what those are?"

Hawk drew himself up with mock pride, he thought. "I do indeed. They are the perfect vehicle for gravy."

They all sat, and he was super proud of Corbin when he handed the knife to Hawk to carve.

Hawk beamed. "Thank you, Corbin." He carved perfect slices of roast beef, and Cosmo thought everyone was impressed. "Now, explain to me video games."

"Okay…this is a challenge. Let's see." Cosmo frowned. "So, they're like movies and games all smooshed together."

Cullen nodded. "And you get to tell the people in the game what to do, but it's all done in the computer, so you can only do what you can do. Like you can invent stuff, but you're playing a game."

Hawk tilted his head. "What kind of game?"

Corbin held his hands open wide. "Man, there are millions of them. All sorts. Puzzles, strategy, first-person shooters. Time management. Old-school. Driving. All sorts."

"And people like them?"

Cosmo nodded to his lover. "Yeah, they're fun. And some of them can even be challenging, but for the most part, they're just fun. You can do them together. You can do them separately. It's very social."

Hawk pursed his lips. "And you're worried about dragon magic manifesting these fake things into reality?"

"Yes. Yes, exactly."

Hawk really was incredibly smart for all of the things he didn't know.

"Well, I can tell you that manifestation magic takes an enormous amount of energy. But I've never seen anyone manifest something into reality that wasn't already, well, in reality." Hawk pulled at his sweater. "This I manifested. I needed clothes. But clothes exist in this realm as a physical thing. I cannot manifest passion. I cannot manifest time. If you have the ability to manifest things, which many of us on the Lunastra can, in my experience, the only things that can be manifested are things that are in reality."

Cosmo stopped for a second. "But guns are real. So, they could manifest guns."

"Yes, if they wanted to," Hawk concurred. "There's precious little need for them, though. We heal from guns, and we manifest food and grow food so we don't need to hunt for food."

"Same with cars. Huh?" Corbin sounded so serious, eyebrows knitted. "I think, that the kids need to be very careful with the video games, Cosmo, don't you?"

"I think that's... I think." He closed his eyes, and he thought about it, hoping that some sort of a vision would come and tell them exactly what to say.

But it didn't.

"I think that their parents have to make this decision, but I think that we need to speak to them. And it is up to us whether we provide anything new."

Cullen blinked. "Can we do that?"

"They made us the guardians. We didn't ask for this job. Guardian doesn't just mean making sure that the bad people don't get in and ruin other lands. It means that human things can't get in to hurt it, and it means that dragon things don't change how it is here. What would happen here if all of a sudden everything started just appearing willy-nilly?"

The vision hit him like a freight train down at the base of his spine, and suddenly, he was transported.

He was thrust into this world where humans could just make things. Magic was rampant and sliding along the ground like thousands and millions of snakes that they couldn't control. These things that didn't belong in that universe. Dragon magic was wild and free and didn't understand constraints. Not like the humans did.

Humans were built to be these creative, exciting, imaginative beings, and to add magic in the mix?

Those in power would just grow and grow and grow with it, and those without would just shrink until they were nothing but minions.

It was an awful thought, and it broke his heart.

He didn't want to see this anymore.

He didn't want to do this anymore.

Hawk's hand touched his shoulder. "Cosmo. Sweet Rose, come back to us. I am here, your brothers are here, and you have supper waiting. All is well."

He could feel his brothers' panic, but Hawk's voice was calm. It was slow and easy and at peace.

The calm made it easier to open his eyes and come back to the dining room where there was Yorkshire pudding and gravy.

And Hawk.

Hawk was right there, those crazy golden eyes just staring into him, keeping him grounded in the now. "There's no way that we're going to let that happen," Hawk said. "We're going to keep magic like that right where it belongs."

"Are you sure? That was awful." Bile was still strong in his throat.

His brothers stared at him too. "What was it?"

"I can't even describe it, it just... It was—Well, it was like an Indiana Jones movie, you know, when the bad guys get a hold of the ark?"

"It's not going to happen, my love. That's why there are Guardians. That's why I'm here with you. I know. It's to be your mate, but it's also to help you guard this gateway. I understand now."

Hawk looked like he understood the universe or something. As if nothing bothered him. And it had to bother him, right? That was why Hawk went to sleep, and he didn't get up, and he didn't know anything beyond what cars were. Because it was overwhelming and because it made him worry. It had to.

But right now, in this place with Cosmo, he seemed so calm, and that made Cosmo feel the same way, as if they could deal with this. As if this was their job, and they were going to be really good at it.

And sometimes, Cosmo hadn't really felt like he was good at anything, so maybe this was his calling. Goddess, he didn't know.

He was just really confused.

"So are we saying that we're not gonna let video games in with the kids?" Cullen asked.

"I'm saying we need to be really careful about what we do let them have, and maybe we need to talk to Sebby and his folks about it. Like when he was living here in this world, it was one thing, but maybe he needs to learn to amuse himself with games and stuff that are from the dragon world, and that way there's no danger."

"I bet once he goes down to school, and he finds more friends, it'll be easier," Cullen suggested.

Corbin shook his head. "I don't know. It could be that it's so much easier to be different, to be the fascinating new kid." They knew from fascinating new kids.

They had been the only half-dragons in their sanctuary. They'd had each other, of course. And, honestly, barring a few assholes, it hadn't been terrible.

Cosmo had to admit that Cullen had especially caught the brunt of the teasing.

Then when they'd left, it had been weirdly like they were never even there.

They were welcome to come home, of course, but only their parents really wanted them. The others seemed confused and suspicious of the fact that they could walk into the human world.

Now that they could walk into the dragonland and back as well? It was this strange situation.

"I didn't think it would be so complicated," Cosmo admitted. "I thought we'd be getting Amazon packages and periodically welcoming the lost dragon in to make sure he was all right before we let him through. Has it always been this hard?"

Hawk shook his head. "Of course not. The last time the veil opened, technology wasn't a thing. We're talking kings and round tables and swords. Knights on horseback. Awful tales of us capturing princesses. Who do you think the guardians were then? When the veil opened that time?"

Cosmo tilted his head. "Was it you?"

Hawk snorted. "Me? No. No, and I wasn't here. I was in the Old Lands back then. The guardians in that time were women. Three mermaid fae crossed. They were triplets called Nimue, Nimnian, and Vivian. They were beautiful, and they were fierce, and they did not allow the evil ones to cross into our home."

Cullen tore apart a Yorkshire pudding and dipped it in his gravy. "How did you get here?"

"I flew. I was bored, and then I was lost. Then when I arrived, I found I enjoyed it here. The seas, the deserts, the mountains—there was so much to see. And no one seemed to mind me. So I stayed. And then I couldn't get back. How about you?"

"Oh, that's an easy one!" Cosmo clapped his hands. "Our father sent us to find his old friend, Gavin, and give him some book that he was searching for. Then Gavin asked us to stay and work for him, and it was so much fun that we did."

It wasn't a fancy story, but it was their story, and it was the truth, so he told it that way.

He seems like he has seen a lot. Corbin murmured, just between them. *I didn't want to like him, but I do.*

He's an old dragon. He's my dragon. He says he doesn't want to go across the veil. He says he wants to stay here with me, and I want to stay here with you.

Corbin nodded, just barely moving his head. *We're glad.*

Maybe that was all his brothers had been worried about. Maybe all the hostility had been because they had been scared he was going to leave them.

Sure, he understood. Hawk was new and different, and he was old. They had assumed that Cosmo would want to go with Hawk, see where Hawk was from. But they were his brothers.

He couldn't leave them anymore than he could stay away from Hawk. Now he was glad he didn't have to do either. His brothers were beginning to understand.

"So what do we do about all this?"

Hawk just smiled. "Well, what we do is we figure out what needs doing."

"Is it really that easy?" Cullen asked.

"Oh, no. It's probably going to be quite difficult, but that's okay. That's what keeps life interesting. When it gets boring, you go to sleep. Or sometimes, it just gets to be too much." That made Hawk frown.

"How do you mean?" Cosmo wanted to reach out and smooth the frown away.

"Things got very loud." Hawk rolled his eyes up toward the ceiling, as if searching for answers. "Things became completely crazy. Everything started moving too fast. I wasn't sure how to keep up, and so I went to sleep. But now? But now I have you. And you understand this new world better than I ever could. Together, we can make this work."

"Do you think that we can keep bad magic from crossing in either direction?" He wanted that vision wiped from his mind.

"I think we can certainly try. I mean, I do have the example of those fierce mermaids, don't I?"

"Yeah, and we have Google."

CHAPTER

NINE

It turned out that there actually had been a series about the last century on this thing they called the History Channel.

Hawk had learned many things in a very short period of time, the main of which was that magic had become something called technology in this world.

That seemed fine. More available than magic and less specific, but fine nonetheless. He approved.

So long as it stayed where it belonged.

The triplets had screens on everything. There were screens that showed pictures of anything you wanted to see. He could see stories and history. He could listen to a book and read a book on a screen. It seemed very odd.

The video games interested him very little, but the puzzles? There were thousands of puzzles that he could do at will anytime he'd like.

That was fascinating.

And he could ask this man, Google, anything, and he would bring up Web books like a library.

He had asked the triplets about this Google person and

his vast library, but they didn't seem to know what the man looked like.

In the deepest part of his brain, Hawk imagined him as an enormous leviathan swimming in this ocean of information, huge tentacles pouring things into different pockets so that one gets it. It was quite the pleasant thought.

Less pleasant was the idea that Cosmo could go out into the dragonland and become hurt, and Hawk couldn't go and rescue him.

Cosmo pointed out, and he told himself as well, that his worries just weren't true. Should something happen to Cosmo on the other side, he could absolutely go in and rescue him.

He just couldn't come back here to his home.

He was curious to meet these dragon children that the triplets told him about, though. And to see how his world had grown and changed in the last millennia.

It was good to be curious. It kept a man alive.

Also concerning was the fact that although they had spent many, many, many hours in bed making wild, passionate love, Cosmo did not seem to be pregnant.

These things took time, of course, and he had no idea how long it took a fae to become with child, but autumn was upon them.

From what he knew of the human lands, it got cold here in the winter, and he wanted Cosmo to be safe. So now maybe he didn't want Cosmo to get pregnant until it was closer to spring. That way, he wouldn't be growing large during the winter months.

"What are you thinking about so hard?" Cosmo asked, coming in to find him scrolling through an electronic book.

"Hmm? Oh, I was simply thinking about information."

Hawk wouldn't mention the pregnancy thing. He didn't want Cosmo to get self-conscious.

"There's a lot of it. I'm proud of you for learning so much."

"Mmmm. Are you? I feel as though I still have a great deal to process." He had watched a movie with Cosmo where the men could put jacks in their head and send the information directly. That might be easier. That way no one had to process it. It was just there as whole knowledge.

"But you just do it. You just soak it all in. It's really cool."

Cosmo bounced a little bit, looking odd.

"What's wrong?" Hawk asked. "What do you need?"

"I know that all of this electronic stuff is super interesting to you right now, but...do you want to go explore? I mean literally, physically, right now. Find a stairwell and go down it and see what's at the bottom."

"I would love that." He was feeling the urge to stretch his legs and to poke his nose into things that it may not belong in. "Where should we start?"

Cosmo grinned hugely. "So, I was in the room underneath the tower room, and I found a secret door."

"Intriguing." He didn't remember a secret door, but that meant very little. "What was in it?"

Cosmo vibrated with his excitement. "I don't know! I was waiting for you. I thought we could go explore it together."

If Hawk hadn't been in love—which he was—he would be now, because that joy?

Was everything.

"Lead the way." All of this screen stuff would be there later. This was the real magic.

Cosmo stood with him, grabbed his hand, and oddly enough, took him to the kitchen.

"Mate?"

"What if we get lost? What if we don't know where we're going? One, we have to make sandwiches and tea. That's a rule."

"Is it?" He was learning so many things.

Cosmo nodded. "The last thing that you need in any given situation is to be hungry or thirsty if you're lost. Also, we're going to bring a piece of chalk so that we can mark our way. That way, we're less likely to get lost."

"You are an incredible explorer."

Cosmo's pink skin warmed. "Thank you, I try. These are the things that we have agreed—the three of us—when we go exploring without each other. It would be a terrible thing to have two in one universe and one in the other and not be able to find each other."

"Oh, my sweet Rosie, that would never happen."

"No?"

"No." Hawk smiled for him. "The three of you are a force of nature. You're meant to be on the same plane no matter what. It's part of the magic of you." He wasn't blowing smoke up Cosmo's ass, either. He meant it. No matter what, the three of them would be together.

"I hope that you're right. Regardless, I think we'll bring chalk." Cosmo grinned at him and winked. "Which sort of sandwiches do you think we should bring?"

He gave that the serious contemplation that it deserved. "Well, we could have cream cheese and cucumber sandwiches."

"I like those." Cosmo pondered. "We could have tuna fish."

"There could be stinky and enclosed places."

Cosmo's eyes lit up. "That's a good point. Let's make peanut butter and jelly. There's blackberry jam."

"Excellent." They cut huge slabs of white bread, slathered them with peanut butter and blackberry for Cosmo, strawberry for him.

Then they wrapped them in paper, put them in a pack with a canister of water. Then they added some chalk that went in their pockets.

"All right, so now—let's find a door." Cosmo took his hand and squeezed. "How did you explore before? Did you just pick a room?"

Had he explored before? Hawk wasn't sure. He didn't particularly remember exploring.

He'd built this house, but he had to admit that even in his wing, some things were just different.

The magic seemed to have been confused when it was recreating the house. Maybe the physical building just didn't fit in the space that the magic needed, and so things got shifted. Maybe he was just really, really old, and he couldn't remember how the hell the place looked to begin with.

"How do you normally do it?"

Cosmo closed his eyes and went very still for a moment. Then he sucked in a quick breath and grinned. "Let's go!"

Then they were off and running, barreling down the hallways like they were children. They made it right to a big door at the end of a hall that he didn't remember having seen there before. "Did this hallway change?"

"Define change."

Hawk fastened Cosmo with a stare. "The definition of change is when something isn't the same as it was only moments before."

"Oh. Then yes. This hallway did change. Let's go. Rawr." Cosmo grabbed the doorknob and yanked it open.

The room Cosmo chose was his library. Oh, glorious. It was still there. The shape of it was different. It had been partially a tower room, so one wall had been rounded, the one with the loft with the walkway and ladders. Now that wall was a straight line, and the balconies were longer and wider, the bookshelves rising a floor higher.

Fascinating.

"Ooh…look at the pretty books!" Cosmo headed for the stacks, eyes alight. "Are they all yours?"

"I think so?" He had no idea. "We should have a look, because who knows?" Hawk chuckled, because Cosmo was already digging in.

Hawk knew what he would find: history, science, magical tomes, and penny dreadfuls. He'd always loved having books to snuggle with of a winter.

"Ohhhh." Cosmo lifted an old leather-bound volume off the shelf. "It's a magical bestiary."

"Is it? How fascinating. Now we need to put it on a table near a sofa so we can read after our explorations."

"Oh, yes. One with a window and a fireplace."

It was as if asking for it made it so. It wasn't. It was much more likely that he knew the nook existed, so his mate saw.

"That sounds perfect. It has to be here somewhere, hmm?"

When they found the couch, tucked away in a nook with a lovely sofa, a table with a tea set just for them, the teapot steaming.

"Look at that!" Cosmo put the book down carefully, keeping it away from the tea and sweets. "Do you have brownies serving your household or something? I haven't met them."

"Or something." When a dragon lived as long as he had, he attracted all sorts of magical beings. Some good, some bad. Brownies, domovoy, nisse...they were all helpful. The boggarts and banshee not so much.

"Oh... Or what? That's exciting. Do you think that they like the fact that you have a mate? Because I'm not going anywhere. In fact, I'm going to be with you forever. I am willing to be friends though. I'd love to be friends."

That he had absolutely no doubt of. Cosmo was quick and friendly, more than willing to reach out.

"Yes, this house has been a place of magic for many, many years. There are many spaces for magical beings to be welcomed. And there are many magical beings in the Lunastra as well."

Cosmo nodded. "It was like that in the Land of Summer, my mother's home. Not many different kinds of magic, but everything there has been touched with light and music, laughter. It's not always happy laughter, though. There can be darkness." Cosmo cuddled into him after pouring them both a cup of tea. "You know, not everyone was happy when my mother mated with my father. Not everyone loves dragons, and not everyone loves the idea of half-breeds."

"That's ridiculous! Half-breeds? That's just...no. You're a special magic all your own. The joining of two magics in love is...well, I simply cannot see that it would be bad."

That wasn't exactly the truth, of course. Hawk could admit to himself he had seen two magics joined together to make a greater, more evil magic.

But this wasn't the time or the place for that nonsense. This was the time to reassure his mate that he found part-fae, part-dragon folk absolutely irresistible.

Especially pink ones.

Most definitely pink ones.

"I know. It's just—Believe me, in a land of very small fae, dragons can seem extremely...large."

"Oh." He leaned back, his teacup in hand. "Yes, I can imagine."

"Right. That bull-in-a-china-shop story has nothing on a dragon in fairyland."

He chuckled. "Oh. I can see that. I mean, nisse are only a foot tall, maybe less. I always worried that I might smoosh them if I was in dragon form." He loved holding Cosmo in his arms, loved having tea and cookies in this little nook.

"So tell me about the nisse."

"They come from the far north. In fact, many believe that's where Santa's elves originated."

"Oh, cool. I mean, I know the rock gnomes live with the Santa Fe clutch. And the Estes clutch has brownies..."

"Yes, you see? When the magic needs to come together, it does."

"Mmm." Cosmo pulled back to look at him. "So wait. Dragon form? Is there a place in your house where you can dragon out? Like be all the way dragon? I want to see you."

"Well, once upon a time, I did. I assume that I still do. I had a basement. It was very deep in the mountain. My hoard was there..."

Cosmo frowned. "Do you have a pool? We really need a pool."

He shook his head. "No, I'm a fire dragon. I really don't care for the water a lot." So, no pool. "There is a sandpit. It's very nice for rolling around in and massaging your scales."

Cosmo tilted his head. "That would be fun. I like sand, I think. I don't see why I wouldn't like sand. Is it warm sand?

Because that sounds...wait. Did it get into, like, weird places?"

He started chuckling. "Not in dragon form that I remember, but it's been a very long time, so perhaps. Perhaps, no, surely not."

"Oh, that's good. That's very good. So we should make a plan to go and search for your sandpit."

"We should. I would like to see your dragon as well."

"I'm not sure about that." Cosmo sort of winced. "We are not the most impressive dragons. I mean, don't get me wrong, we are magical and clever and quick, but not particularly impressive."

"No?" Now Hawk was curious. "Can you explain?"

"I'm sure I could, but I really don't want to." Cosmo rolled his eyes. "You see...well, one, we're half fae, and two, we're half dragon, and three, there's three of us and so... To be perfectly honest, if you put all three of our dragons together, we're not the size of a whole dragon. We're little. Like, *little.*"

Hawk frowned. "How little is little?" He held his fingers about six inches apart. "Little?"

"Here." Cosmo's sighed and rolled his eyes. Then suddenly, immediately, instead of a man, he held a lean, perfectly formed, very, very little dragon. He was exactly the size of Cosmo as a man. Pink and sparkling.

Hawk was absolutely stunned.

I told you I wasn't a very impressive dragon.

His mouth opened and closed, then opened and closed again. He simply couldn't speak.

At least not until he could feel Cosmo pulling away, then he found his voice again.

"Oh my rose, you're beautiful." He'd never seen

anything or anyone more perfect in all of his life. "Such a lovely dragon."

He ran his fingers down along Cosmo's scales. He found them cool and smooth, and he swore he could hear music as he petted the long spine. "The tip of your tail is shaped like a heart."

The tip of Cosmo's tail was shaped like a heart.

Hawk couldn't be more in love if he tried.

You don't think I look strange? Cosmo asked.

"Of course not. I think you're amazing." He couldn't believe how stunning Cosmo was. He had never seen such a thing in his life, and he'd had a pretty long life.

Cosmo ducked his head, just snuggled in. *I wanna be amazing for you.*

"Oh, love, you're perfect. Now shall we read our book and have our tea?" Maybe they just needed to relax together.

Cosmo nodded, his head dipping again. *I think that's a wonderful idea.*

So Hawk grabbed the book. And they read about magical beasts. And had tea. Careful not to spill it on the book, of course. And Hawk thought that Cosmo relaxed. He would have to think about this, about how to make Cosmo understand that he was wonderful, magical. And his.

CHAPTER

TEN

Cosmo sat in the living room, not sure what he should do. Hawk was still asleep. Not the kind of sleep that he worried Hawk would slip into, just normal sleep. But no one was up yet. And Cosmo wanted to... He didn't know. Play cribbage? Watch a movie with somebody?

Just talk to his brothers about how it had been to be in his dragon form with Hawk and not be mocked for it. Oh, the dragons that they knew on the other side of the house, the Rocky Mountain clutch, had never mocked them. Neither had the people in their village down in Lunastra. But he knew they were something of a novelty.

Hawk just seemed as though he accepted Cosmo for what he was, and that was strange. It caused all sorts of feelings in his chest, and he didn't know how to deal with them.

All of this was new. This whole bonding was nuts, and he just...felt like he really was, well, he was gonna explode. Maybe. Who knew?

Just when he thought he was going to get up and run

laps around the house, Corbin came downstairs, hunting something in the kitchen. So Cosmo got up and wandered along behind him. Maybe he'd have a Coke, or maybe he wouldn't. He didn't know.

Corbin looked at him. "Are you okay? You seem… restless."

"I think I am. I don't know what to do about Hawk."

"What about him? I thought you were like all over the thing with him. Like super happy."

"I am, and I'm not gonna get rid of him or anything. I mean. I love him so much already, but I just—don't know how to deal with some of the stuff that's going on in my head. You know?"

"Wait, you have a brain?"

"Oh, shut up, you asshole." He frowned thunderously, and Corbin held his hands up.

"Joking. Joking. Wow, you're really caught up in this guy, if you can't take a joke."

"Well, I am. I mean, I really am!" And he found himself dangerously close to tears, which really pissed him off. He threw one hand up and stormed to the fridge. "Never fucking mind, I'm fine. I just need a drink."

There was silence from behind him, and Cosmo was going to have an absolute temper tantrum if his brother just walked off and left him when he was in a snit and didn't even say he was sorry or anything, when familiar arms wrapped around him, hugging him tight.

"Dude, I'm sorry. I didn't realize that it was this big."

Not bad. Corbin hadn't said bad, and that was a huge jump forward for his stubborn brother.

"It really is. You don't understand. He's willing to stay here and never cross over just to be with me because I want to be with you both."

"Well, you know that if you needed to..." Corbin couldn't even finish the sentence before Cosmo was shaking his head.

"But we all know I can't. None of us can. This isn't about what we wanted. No one ever asked us. You do understand that, right? No one asked us because we never had a choice. We were always going to be the next Guardians."

"Did Hawk tell you that?"

"No. No, but I'm not stupid. I have enough sense to know when I hear the stories about the other guardians of the other places—when they were all half dragon and half something else, or half something and half something else and there was always three of them—Aren't you listening?"

Corbin stared at him. "Yeah. I'm listening."

"Aren't you mad?"

Cosmo was, and he wasn't even sure absolutely one hundred percent why, but he knew he was mad.

Possibly because nobody had given them any choice and warned them, even though there really wasn't anybody to warn them, because they'd already been stuck in this job before Hawk was there to explain to them what the history was so that he could figure out that they were fucked.

Cullen came down, frowning. "What the hell are you guys screaming about?"

"I'm not screaming." Corbin pointed out. "That's Cosmo. He's very angry."

"Obvi. What the fuck is going on?"

"None of you are listening to me! We've trapped Hawk here. Completely by accident."

"No, we haven't. Nobody did anything. He can go."

Cosmo was going to hit Cullen in the face. Bang.

It was less fun than normal to hit Cullen in the face

because, well, he was already purple. So when he bruised, he just sort of got a little darker. It wasn't particularly colorful, so that wasn't near as satisfying, but the sound, just the sound of going whack—

"No hitting." Corbin sighed. "I really think you need a drink."

"I really do." Cosmo sat down in one of the kitchen chairs. Hard.

"I got you." Cullen went to the fridge to pull out milk, then grabbed the Mexican hot chocolate stuff. Oh. Hot cocoa would be good.

"Adult hot chocolate," Cullen said into the void. "That's appropriate for this time of the morning. I'll spike it with that vanilla vodka."

"Yum." He blinked, trying to push aside some of the adrenaline and the worry and the—the rage. Which had come out of nowhere.

Love, are you well? Hawk seemed to be tapped into his moods, just like his brothers would be.

I don't know. Cullen is making hot chocolate.

I'll be down in a moment. Can you warn your brothers?

Of course. "Hawk is on his way down."

"I'll make pancakes." Corbin ruffled his hair. "It's going to be okay, bro. I promise."

"How?"

"I dunno. It's a mystery."

"Okay, yeah." He chuckled. Corbin loved to paraphrase his favorite movies when he was stressed. "But maple syrup will help."

"Maple syrup is proof that there is a greater power, and that she loves us," Cosmo admitted. "I'm sorry, guys."

He shrugged, pulling into himself. He wasn't sure what the hell was going on inside of him, but there were all of these horrible feelings that just wouldn't stop, wouldn't cease their endless bubbling and colliding. It was ridiculous.

I'm afraid that's partially me. Rosie. Hawk's voice was a gentle touch, but so different than his brothers', so much bigger.

Your fault?

I've been around a very long time. And I can be moody.

Well, are you moody now? I mean, are you unhappy?

No. I've been waiting for you for millennia. How could I be unhappy? I have my mate.

Cosmo had to smile because honestly all he did feel from Hawk's mental voice was happiness. Hawk didn't regret being stuck here, at least not yet. In fact, he was happy to have Cosmo.

Still, someone should have told him about the whole Guardian thing. Someone should have warned them.

"I don't think that anyone knew," Corbin said, answering his unspoken worries. "I still don't understand about this whole warning thing. I know that I'm slow, but can you explain?"

Hawk came rolling in wearing a pair of bright yellow pants that looked like bananas, along with a purple velvet smoking jacket.

Interesting sartorial choices. Cosmo liked it.

"Let me see if I can explain," Hawk said. "Over the millennia—as far as I know, and I would assume as far as most anyone knows—when the veil opens, there has always been a set of triplets who were the product of two magical species. They've guarded the connection between the worlds, allowing the very few stragglers in and out as it needed to happen. And protecting these separate spaces from one another. It seems like that you three got the job."

"Well, that's not too bad, is it?" Cullen asked. "I mean, we like this house. We like each other. Hawk's okay. We get to go all over. Where's the bad?"

"Well, the bad is they didn't—"

The vision took him in a rush, and suddenly, all he could see were oceans of blood. The entire world turned red and sticky. The smell of copper everywhere and flashing teeth and ruby eyes and anger. Just this awful, empty, mindless anger.

No, no, that wasn't anger.

It was hunger.

Cosmo knew someone was talking to him, but he really couldn't hear what was going on. All he could do was let the vision have him until it was done. He hoped that whatever he was seeing was just a product of his dour mood about being a guardian, but he didn't think so.

These waves of prescience happened, and then, sooner or later, something came along to prove that his talent really was seeing what was going to happen in the future. Cosmo really wished he had a better talent, something that wasn't going make him utterly insane one of these days.

Maybe that was why Hawk was there. He didn't know.

When he snapped back to himself, his eyes rolling back down out of his head, Hawk was holding him. He'd fallen out of his chair, he thought.

"What did you see?" Cullen asked.

It was pretty obvious that he was having a vision, he guessed. There was no getting away with saying oh, I just kind of had a seizure or something.

Cosmo blinked, trying to figure out how to put into words what he had seen. And what he'd felt. "It was all red," he said. "And hunger. It was awful."

Hawk held him closer, lending strength and heat, which was lovely, but Cosmo couldn't shake the vision.

Corbin stared into his eyes. "What kind of hunger? What are you talking about?"

"Well, if I knew. It would be useful, wouldn't it? It was toothy, whatever it was, and it was coming for us. It's something that we have to guard against, and maybe that's why I've been feeling so uneasy."

"That's it, I'm buying garlic."

"What?" Cosmo was nowhere near unrattled enough to follow whatever the hell Corbin was talking about.

"Vampires. This place was attacked by vampires. Infested with vampires. They killed two dragons here. It hasn't been that long. We were still cleaning the blood out of the wood not long ago. You can still smell dragon blood in my side of the house!" Corbin was just getting warmed up. "I'm buying garlic—cases of it. And crosses. Can you buy holy water?"

"I'll look it up," Cullen said. "I can get sun lamps too. I wonder if they make portable sun lamps?"

Hawk growled low. "Vampires. Soulless creatures. We're infinitely more satisfying to them than humans. They cannot be allowed through the veil."

"Well, I guess that that's our job then, to sit here and let them suck on us and bleed us dry so that they can't get through the veil." Cosmo didn't like this at all.

"Oh, bullshit. We're going to cover this entire house on the front end with roses, a la the Sleeping Beauty myth. Big thorny roses everywhere—we'll leave a door for the Amazon delivery and groceries. Then we will just put garlic wreaths everywhere." Corbin was going on and on, and Cosmo dropped his head in his hands.

Then he lifted it and sighed. "If you don't stop him, he's

going to start inventing handheld sun lamp ray gun things. I know." He put his head back down again. Then lifted it. "I've seen it."

"Oh, ray guns are cool." Hawk held him, rocked him, and smiled at Corbin. "I think we should research what is fact and what is fiction before we start just buying many of one sort of item. No worries, though. I do know one thing."

Cosmo looked up at Hawk. "What's that, mate?"

"There's never been a vampire born that could withstand lava."

CHAPTER
ELEVEN

Hawk watched with bemusement over the next few weeks as Cosmo and Cullen and Corbin fortified the house.

Corbin grew roses at an alarming rate. They were beautiful and healthy, but large and thorny. And they took up the entire front of the house. What didn't get covered in roses got covered in ivy and other vines that worked their way into the stones, into the wood, and strengthened everything.

Cullen practiced illusions. Practiced hiding the entire house, which was a lovely trick, but would not particularly fool a vampire. It did panic Corbin at one point when he returned from the greenhouse to find the house gone...

Cosmo. Well, Cosmo worried him. Cosmo looked pale and sad and not at all rosy like he should. Hawk wanted to tell him not to borrow trouble; if the vampires came, they would come. Why work oneself into a frenzy if it wasn't going to happen?

And he'd meant what he said. There wasn't a vampire on

earth who could withstand a flow of lava. Now, that didn't mean that he wouldn't burn the house down, but such trade-offs were required sometimes. He hoped that wouldn't happen, but they could always rebuild, he supposed.

Instead of letting Cosmo mope around for the rest of the day, Hawk was going to tempt his lover into exploring more of the house. They hadn't done that since the lovely day that they had spent having tea and cookies in the library, but now he wanted to find the sandpit. He really wanted to get his scales polished, and he wanted to teach Cosmo how wonderful that was as well. It really did a mind and body good.

He started his seduction, so to speak, with long stretching. and low moaning, and stealing a peek at his mate to see if perhaps his Cosmo had noticed.

No.

He pursed his lips and really stretched again, longer this time, arms going wide.

When that didn't get a response, he huffed out a breath that smelled vaguely reminiscent of brimstone.

"Are you all right?" Cosmo came hurrying over, expression concerned. "Is everything all right?"

"Oh, mate." He sighed. "I itch. I itch most terribly."

"It's all right, I'll scratch you. Here." Cosmo held out his hands, and Hawk shook his head.

"No, no, no. I was wondering... I have tea and lovely sandwiches and cookies and chalk already in the bag. I have the urge to explore."

A hint of light lit up his mate's eyes, and he was on the right track. "Are you sure it's safe?"

"Absolutely not. It could be incredibly naughty. Let's go down to the basement." He went for his best grin, which could at times be considered incredibly toothy. Thank goodness Cosmo loved him.

"Oh, the basement. Do you think we could go right now? Would be so nice to just do something rather than... nothing."

He held up his little pack. He hadn't put it together, of course. His wonderful housemates had, but it was all meant well. He'd asked for it. "We could go right now."

Then he held out his hand, and he was so pleased when Cosmo's fingers twined with his. They were warm, the touch solid for the first time in days. Present.

They didn't even tell Corbin and Cullen where they were going, but they didn't have to.

The triplets were eternally bonded, and there was absolutely no doubt they could feel Cosmo's excitement, his eagerness to go wander.

The big basement door was in the kitchen, and he pulled it open, laughing as it made it horrific screech.

"No matter how many times I oil this door," he told Cosmo. "It makes this noise. I think it's haunted."

Cosmo peered at the door, taking specific interest in the hinges. "I think perhaps you're right, at least partially. More inhabited and less haunted. It seems as if there may be a tiny sprite living inside the upper hinge."

"Well, I'll stop pouring oil into your home," he yelled toward the door, and he swore he heard a tiny—

"That would be much appreciated."

His Cosmo was handy as a pocket on a shirt.

They wandered down the big stairs, which were nowhere near as terrifying as one would think basement stairs ought to be. They were wide and stone and suitable for a dragon who might have to shift in very close quarters, especially a very big dragon, and so it was quite the easy wander down.

The walls were covered in tapestries to warm everything a bit. There were some images of dragons, some of mighty towers, some familial crests.

But for the most part, they were bucolic landscapes.

Hawk liked the idea of the sun being down in the basement and flowers and growing things. Not that things in the dark didn't grow, but for the most part, they could be unpleasant.

"These are beautiful," Cosmo told him. "I don't remember them being here when I peeked in."

"No, no, that basement is the not-me basement."

"The not-you basement?" Cosmo chuckled softly.

"Yes, it takes a certain will, if you would like, to see my basement. The other basement is more for show. Like a pretend basement. It's quite dank, and I let odd things grow there. It discourages too much investigation."

Cosmo rolled with his laughter. "I like it."

"Thank you, my love. I thought it was rather clever." He smiled and bounced, because it was all brand new, showing things to Cosmo. In all honesty, some of it was new to him anyway. There were so many things that were different, but he knew where they were going. Vaguely.

Hawk led Cosmo down a large flagstone hallway. The walls were covered in more tapestries, and as they got farther down, the stones warmed under their feet. Like most dragon hideouts, his had a geothermal pocket to it. It didn't have hot springs, but it did have the handy sandpit.

He really did enjoy that. He could smell the vaguely sulfurous smell that one usually associated with mineral waters. But in this case, it would be the heat rising off the sand, so they had to be close.

"Oh, wow. I can smell that," Cosmo told him. "That's kind of amazing."

Hawk nodded eagerly. "I know. Somewhere down on the other side of all of that is my hoard."

"Really? I need to see that too. But first, I want to scrub your scales. I know you said you itch."

"I do. And I also want a picnic with you. It's just fun."

Cosmo laughed. And it was so good to hear. He'd been so down. Hawk didn't want his love to be sad. He wanted him to be happy that they were together, and he wanted to be able to provide that happiness.

Swinging his hand, Cosmo was almost running now, and they tumbled through the halls. A warren of mazelike, although not small, corridors. He had spent a great deal of time as a dragon instead of a man over the years, and he'd designed things so that he could move around and also so that he could defend his home.

Stone burned way less than wood or even glass. It took much hotter temperatures to make it melt, after all. And it was way easier to scrub the soot off, and also whatever other sorts of things might be left after a battle. Hence Cullen saying that he still had blood to scrub out of his part of the house. Hawk had a feeling that was mostly wood considering that was part of the A-frame.

Wood fibers just drank up the blood. It was never going to get all the way out.

Cosmo wandered with him, floating around to explore the things that he had hidden—a gemstone here, a little statue in a niche there. He hadn't thought at the time that he was hiding them to amuse his mate, but magic worked in mysterious ways.

Perhaps he had been, and he just hadn't known it.

They wandered until they got down to the sandpit, the

staircase opening up to a huge room that was lit by dozens of huge stones that glowed with enclosed magma, the walls shiny obsidian, reflecting the light and fragmenting it.

"Oh... Oh, look, love—" Cosmo sounded absolutely stunned, and that pleased him down to the core. This was more than his house. This space was his heartbeat, his center, and the fact that his mate thought it was beautiful honored him deeply.

"You like it? I've worked on it for many, many years until it was just the way I wanted it." He took a deep breath, let it out in a sigh. "It's been a while since I've been here. I can tell there's a little dusting needs to be done."

"A little bit, but it's doable. Are the rocks hot?"

"Warm, yes, but they won't burn you." There is no way that he could burn his mate. He knew it.

"Oh, sound good. Let's get to work."

And there was some work to be done. The random cobweb the size of a truck, a few critters that needed encouragement to move, and the periodic lump of glass that he created when he fell asleep in the sandpit and snored. That was always such a challenge. It did make for interesting sculptures in the house, though.

Cosmo picked one of the rather large pieces of glass up, tilting his head. "This is fascinating. Are the little drip parts on the side where you drooled lava?"

"Don't make me beat you." He laughed, his entire self cracking up, because not only was it funny, but it was basically true. He wasn't sure—he'd been asleep.

Cosmo carefully took the pieces of glass to the side of the pit, arranging them like a little army. "They're beautiful. I like them."

Hawk gave Cosmo a sideways glance. "You do?"

"Of course I do. They're manifestations of you." He got a sparkling grin. "Now food or naked first?"

"Mmmm. Food. It will be better in this form. When I get naked and in the sand, I'm liable to go big on you, and then these tidbits will be too small." Hawk waved a hand. "And I wish to enjoy our snack together."

"Ah. Well, then." Cosmo beamed. "Let's have some nibbles."

"Yes, let's." Hawk picked his way across the sand to an area where Cosmo could sit, brushing it off a little and putting down a blanket. That would make it nicer for when they ate.

He unpacked the repast the brothers had made for him, humming, because he approved. Sandwiches. Fruit. Cookies. Water, and a thermos of tea. How lovely and civilized.

He poured the tea into the provided mugs, which were some unbreakable material. Very 1950s.

"So, tell me more about your home," he asked Cosmo, teasing.

His rose looked at him, confused. "This is my home."

Hawk chuckled, tickled pink—pun intended. "No, I mean where you grew up. Tell me something about it that I don't know."

Cosmo shrugged. "It's always summer. It's always beautiful. The sun always shines and the flowers bloom. Everyone is beautiful. Perfect. To be honest, it's kind of boring. I mean it's not as...pat as all that, but it is peaceful and simple. You are born in the class that you're born in. You stay there. You have education, and you learn the things that you're supposed to learn. I can't even say that I was isolated, because I had my brothers—so while there might only be three dragon-fae mixes in the summer land, there were three of us. And my father doesn't seem too unhappy."

"No?" Hawk was intrigued. "So he went there to be with her?"

"He did. He couldn't bear the idea of losing his lover, and he couldn't stand the idea of not seeing his children grow up." Cosmo leaned hard into him, sipping his tea. "She was out here in this world when she got pregnant. I think she'd come to give Dad some sort of a warning? You know, watch out, the mountain's gonna explode. Vesuvius was a little tricksy in those day, you know. But instead of going back home, she stuck around, I guess."

"Oh my. That's fascinating. Also, she was pregnant when she went home?"

Cosmo nodded. "Yeah. And then, when they wouldn't let Dad come, she went to him and threatened to stay in the human world forever and raise her babies. So they changed the rules and let him in."

"Is he happy?"

"He seems to be pretty satisfied. He makes things, and he takes care of Mom and gardens and lets her boss him around. It's kind of adorable. Sweet."

"And they never had any more children."

Cosmo shook his head. "No. They never came back out into the human world, and I guess that's how that works. When they come out into this place where the magic is wild and untamed, they can do that thing, and then, boom. You get us."

And thank goodness for that. "I can't think of anything I'd want more."

Cosmo widened his eyes. "Hey, now. Cullen and Corbin and I are practically perfect in every—"

"Yes, yes. That line, I know." He handed Cosmo a sandwich. "I just mean that your brothers are very protective. I'm not sure I would wish to contend with even more of that." He gave Cosmo a warm look. "You, I adore."

"As you should," Cosmo said promptly, then flushed again, laughing. "I'm just giving you shit."

"What on earth would I want with shit?" He tried, and failed, to keep a straight face.

"Don't make me beat you." Cosmo popped a piece of sandwich into his mouth, effectively shutting him up. "At some point, I'm sure that my mother will pop out and see us. Dad never leaves anymore. He used to, but I haven't seen him do it in forever."

Curious. "No? Why?"

"Politics. What if they decide once he leaves that they wouldn't let him come back? He and Mom are a thing. They couldn't do without each other. Like I said, he's pretty happy. He makes his wood creatures and potters around in the garden, and... They make each other laugh."

"We should all hope for something so wonderful."

"Well, fortunately for you, you have it." Cosmo threw his arms open with a happy laugh, wrinkling his nose playfully. "I am hilarious."

"You're beautiful, and I want to get all dragony with you and wallow in the sand." Hawk craved it, even.

"I can do that. First, though, let me polish your scales. It's going to feel so good."

They put the food away carefully, and both stripped down, heading into the sand, the black dust sliding under their feet. It was perfectly smooth, silken as they walked.

"It gets warmer toward the middle," he warned. "In fact, in the very center, it's almost hot."

Cosmo hummed and nodded. "Noted. Good for scales, not so good for skins, is that what you're saying?"

"Exactly."

Cosmo took a kiss, hand sliding down his back, and then they both knelt on the sand. It was so tempting just to stop here and make love.

But honestly, in their human form, sand did get into the most inconvenient places, and that could chafe. Not only that, they always could make love afterward.

He was aching to resume his true form again.

"Ready?" he asked, not wanting to startle Cosmo.

"I am."

He closed his eyes and let his dragon form take him. It came on with a whoosh of magic, and he felt the rush of it, his laughter ringing off the walls and the ceiling.

Cosmo chuckled, and when Hawk opened his eyes, there was a beautiful rose dragon there with him, little and bright and shining.

Love. He nuzzled Cosmo's snout, his head at least three times the size of his mate's.

Look at you, Cosmo told him. *You're huge. At least as big as Dad. Maybe bigger.*

Hawk preened. *Is that a good thing?*

That's an amazing thing. Cosmo picked up two great paws full of sand and began scrubbing his back.

Hawk was going to die from pure, indescribable joy.

Mate and hot sand and rubbing?

And he was home, and he could hear his hoard, and life was so good that the only thing that could make it better was if they were going to have a baby.

Wait.

They had sex a lot. Like quite a lot, and he'd been here for a goodly number of months.

Surely, they'd touched on one nexus of the year or another, right? Surely, it was so.

Still, Cosmo didn't seem to be pregnant. There was no grumbling about food or strange smells or anything baby related. Not to mention, he would know if that little belly swelled, because it was a tiny little belly, especially as a dragon. He would see.

He would know.

Maybe...maybe dragon fae didn't have babies? That would be a shame.

Absolutely not a deal breaker, however.

If he had a choice between Cosmo or many babies, he would take Cosmo every single time.

He was hoping, however, that at some point the situation would be Cosmo *and* babies, but if not, that was all right.

He could live with that.

He'd lived without babies forever.

Perhaps one had to be older than him. Hmm. It didn't matter.

There would be babies or there wouldn't.

Right now, there was sand and rubbing.

Cosmo was exceptional at knowing exactly where each and every individual itch was. He had never had anyone go over his body scale by scale, rubbing in the sand and making sure that nothing itched.

He was going to spend the rest of eternity making this dragon unbearably happy just so they could do this again.

Cosmo was singing, the song merry and soft, just floating through the air. He didn't know the words or the song, but it didn't matter.

He knew what was underneath it.

He knew what was inside it.

Joy.

CHAPTER

TWELVE

The sandpit was the coolest thing in a long history of cool things. Well, it was actually really hot, but it was Hawk hot, and it hadn't burned him. Not even when they'd fallen asleep.

Of course, he kinda fit into one of Hawk's paws, didn't he. Well, not really, but into the crook of his dragon front arm, yes.

Wallowing in hot sand. Who knew? It was an amazing thing.

And it had eased his worry. Made it better.

"Where have you been?" Corbin asked him while he was making dinner, humming this song he could only hear in his head. Cosmo was starting to think of it as Hawk's song. Like their mating tune. Who knew?

"Hawk's volcanic sandpit."

"His what?" Corbin stared at him. "Get out."

"Tis true." He winked. "Instead of a pool, he has sand." Cosmo held out one hand. "I'm glowing, see? Very good for the scales."

"You're shitting me."

"Nope." He shook his butt a little, the song swelling. Hawk must be on his way.

In fact, Hawk came into the room just after that.

"Tell him, babe."

Hawk raised his eyebrows. "Tell him what?"

"About the sand."

"It's a pit? Actually, it's more like volcanic glass sand. It's black, super smooth, perfect for polishing."

Corbin blinked, expression hungry. "Dude, I'm jealous."

"Whyever for?" Hawk smiled at him. "We're family. You're welcome anytime."

Cosmo could feel his brother's shock, could see the hint of surprise. "Really?"

"Yes, brother. Really."

"Thank you." Corbin offered Hawk a quick smile, then peered into the pot, where he was making a vegetable soup from the last of the late summer bounty. "I think the pumpkins are almost ready to harvest. It's been an incredible crop."

"Oh, pumpkin pie, pumpkin soup, pumpkin bread. Just roasted pumpkin." Cosmo rubbed his hands together, very excited.

"Yum."

"I have a good recipe for pumpkin curry." Hawk began to talk food with Corbin, and he loved to see it.

Things seemed to be easier this evening. He wasn't quite sure if it was because he was relaxed or because things were simply going to be better with Hawk and his brothers as time went on. He wanted everyone to love Hawk like he did.

Well, not exactly like he did...

Cullen's laughter tickled his mind. *We do love him, goofball.*

I know, I just. "Is it weird to you too?" he burst out at the exact moment as Cullen walked in.

"Is what weird to us too?"

"There's no work. I mean there is housework, but there are no jobs. Gavin's not sending us anywhere. There is precious little beginning, middle, or end? It's just one long story."

It was Corbin who nodded first. "It is weird. Less for me, I think, than for the two of you, because at least I get growing season, harvest season, fallow season. Beginning, middle, end. Inside the house like this, there aren't any."

Hawk gave them all a sad little smile. "That is how life works. You do know that?" He softened the words with a smile and a blown kiss to Cosmo. "We have this timeline, and we wander along it inventing, building beginnings, middles, and ends."

Cosmo shook his head. "No, we're not simply inventing. We didn't make up *our* beginning. And the end won't come until it's both of us together. All of us. That's an eternity away."

Hawk came to him, hugged him. "You do know if you want to go back to work, I would come with you?"

Cosmo stared at Hawk. "Love. You can't just wander out in the human world. You are kind of intensely dragony. Cullen could cover you, but if something happened, and he slipped? Whoa. It would be a nightmare."

Hawk tilted his head, eyebrows drawing down. "What do you mean?"

Cosmo stroked Hawk's forehead. "Up here. Scales." He kept touching. "Eyes, dragon. Arms. Belly. You're very drag-ony, love."

Hawk looked shocked. "I suppose since I don't have to hold a certain form..."

Cosmo nodded. "Right. Just like I'm really pink. I could be not pink, but it takes some energy. Honestly, though, I like being pink."

He loved getting his dragon on.

"I love you being pink too." Hawk winked at him, and Cosmo had to grin because he could see the care in Hawk's eyes. "But I understand what you mean about us not going out."

"No. It's not like I won't take you out. It just means that we have to be careful about it." Cosmo figured there were just a few logistics involved.

Hawk shook his head. "I'm perfectly content here. I just don't want you to be unhappy, love. You or your brothers. If we need to have some sort of ceremony to make it where there's a beginning, middle, and end to the years, we could start celebrating the holidays? We've let several go by, I think, without notice since I came. Is that something that you do?"

"We've never celebrated the human holidays completely because we don't really know them as well, I suppose. But that could be fun." Cosmo liked the idea of like, decorating. He would get on Pinterest.

Corbin nodded. "We could get a calendar. We could do all sorts of stuff. I kind of like that idea. You know, weird holidays. They have all sorts of things now, like. Bring your dog to work day. That kind of weirdness."

Cosmo blinked at Corbin. "We don't really have dogs."

"Well, we could." Corbin laughed out loud. "I mean, a lot of dragons we know have familiars."

Cullen shook his head. "No, but those familiars show up on their own. We don't do that."

Hawk tilted his head to one side. "I seem to remember having a familiar once. Not the way that omegas do when they have babies, but I do remember it. That was a long time ago. I think it was a big cat."

"Really? What kind?"

"Oh, I imagine it was something amazing brought over from Africa. Something no one had ever seen back then."

"That's really cool. I mean, not that somebody would take a lion away from their family and take it to Europe. But that you know all about how it happened. The story behind it." Cosmo had never felt as anchored in history as Hawk.

"I know all sorts of things, my love. If you think really hard on it and decide that you want a familiar, then one will show up."

"Is that how it happens?"

"Well," Hawk mused, "it can also work when someone in the family is having a baby and then the familiar is needed to help take care of the children, but that's not the only reason they show up. It's just like a brownie or another house spirit. When they're needed, they come."

"Do you really think so?" That was kind of an intriguing thought. He loved the idea of having more friends to enjoy, more beings to interact with.

It wasn't as if he was bored.

There was so much to do and so much to learn, and he had Hawk. He just felt unrooted, like it wouldn't take anything to just spin them away into nothingness. That was an uncomfortable way to live.

"Well, when you get pregnant, someone will come, right, Cosmo?" Cullen acted as if it was just a simple and easy answer.

"Well, I think it's more an if than a when, isn't it?" He wasn't pregnant now, and it wasn't like they hadn't been very, very busy.

"Oh. I suppose you're right. Maybe we can't get pregnant…" Cullen started creating balls of rainbow-colored light and juggling them.

"Maybe I don't want to," he shot back.

"You don't have to," Hawk growled.

"Of course you don't. Cullen was just being a dipshit." Corbin patted his arm before pulling him into a hug and squeezing him tight. "We have plenty to do without babies being involved."

"Absolutely," Cullen agreed, balls splashing to the ground. "Totally. So much. So many things. All the things we need to do, right?" Cullen gave him a worried, apologetic little smile. *Oh, I'm so sorry. I didn't mean to hurt your feelings, not at all.* "I really think that I walked into this conversation in the middle of everything. Should I make bread? Or something?"

"Or something. There's bread already." *You're fine, brother. I'm just…it's sad.* He forced himself to shake off any tension. "No one's in trouble. It's weird. That we're—I mean, the dragons get pregnant all the time."

"Well, not Brandon," Corbin pointed out. "Brandon had to have a little help."

"Right, Stella, the owl baby." *Beautiful little clever girl.*

Hawk looked like they were speaking a foreign language. "Stella the owl baby?"

Cosmo nodded, heading over to pull out some soup bowls. "Yes. Apparently, Brandon was having problems conceiving."

Cullen made a sad sound. "And he wanted to have a baby so badly, and after a lot of time…"

"Zeke talked to Auntie Arian," Corbin added.

"He did, and Brandon got pregnant, but she's not exactly a dragon like her fathers." *Not that Brandon and Abe cared. Not at all.*

"In fact, she's sort of an owl." Cullen suddenly grew feathers.

"Like a literal owl?" It said something that Hawk didn't even flinch at Cullen.

"Oh no. She's..." How to explain?

"She's very, very special." Cullen spread his fingers and there was Stella, tiny and perfect and brilliant, but absolutely not dragonkind.

"Oh." Hawk seemed fascinated.

"But he's only had the one baby," Corbin explained. "And they're both perfectly happy."

"And I'm perfectly happy without any babies." Mostly. It was really weird that he couldn't have babies. But he was happy.

Hawk pulled him close, kissing his temple. "I am happy with you no matter how we do it, love." *And I should never have brought up babies. Your brothers are...very concerned.*

They are. But that's just because they love me.

Mmm. So do I. Hawk nuzzled his cheek.

Corbin gave them a look. "Do you need to go get a room?"

"Nope. We're going to have hot chocolate. And maybe cinnamon toast. That's something you can make, Cullen."

"Woo." Cullen got to work slicing bread, and he turned the conversation to something else.

The last thing Cosmo wanted was to make everyone else as restless and weird as he was...

THIRTEEN

Hawk wandered around the house a little, feeling as though he needed to…do something. He wasn't sure what it was, but something was pushing at him.

He could feel it, pressing against him like the weight of too much volcanic ash after a long nap. It made him want to shake it off, to burn the worry away.

So he did what he usually did in such situations. He went to the library.

Oh, he often went to his hoard, too, but right now, he couldn't find it, so this was his option. Perhaps he would research dragon and fae hybrids.

He got to the library and sat his coffee on one of the big tables so it wouldn't get spilled on the books. Then he began his search.

He was perhaps an hour in when he heard, "Psst."

He blinked. "Yes?"

"Hawk. It has been a long while, my friend."

"Ah, Bakli. Hello, my old friend. It has been a long time."

The little nisse crawled out of a book nook, his long white beard tucked into his tunic. "It has. Too long."

"Have you been well? They've been feeding you?"

"It has been very quiet, very lonely. We were pleased to find habitants rambling about, and even more pleased when we discovered it was your mate. We were waiting for you to come home."

"Oh." Hawk was happy they'd known Cosmo was his. That made him feel even better, because while he hadn't worried honestly about whether or not Cosmo had been his, it was always good to have validation.

"Things have changed very much since I was here last."

"Oh, yes. The veil has opened and closed. The world's magic...well, we are in between that, aren't we? This is In Between." He loved how Bakli said the word in capital letters.

In Between.

"We are. It is an important space."

He got the most serious look. "A terribly important space. This is one of the spaces where the worlds meet, a grand nexus. An In Between, and it is very important that we keep the balance here."

He nodded, acknowledging his friend's words. "The balance among the worlds is delicate, yes. Even one as large as I am can tell that."

Bakli gave him a warm smile. "I'm glad. It pleases us, all of us that you have decided to support the guardians in this."

"Do you foresee there being attacks on this home?"

Bakli nodded. "Yes, this is not a stable space yet. It is new, and because of that and because of history, the magics here are like a beacon." He shrugged. "Unfortunately, beacons don't simply work one way. You need the dragons who are lost to find their way here. You want the magical beings who are lost to find their way home. You do not want an infestation."

The way that Bakli wrinkled his nose in distaste brought the vampires immediately to mind.

He could only imagine how much power the vampires could possibly have in the dragonlands.

"We will guard against that while letting those who need to pass through." He gave the vow with the best of intentions, all the while knowing that the best intentions could fail sometimes. So, he needed to be conscious. "I am awake now, and I will be on watch."

"So will we, my friend."

"Good, good. Do you know where my hoard is, Bakli?"

Bakli chuckled. "I do. But that is not what you want to know right now."

He tilted his head. True enough. He wanted to know why Cosmo was not with child. And while he was truly happy to be with Cosmo no matter what, since he'd brought it up, he could tell it was preying on Cosmo's mind a bit.

"It took very much magic to create this space, and I do not believe that your mate and his brothers understand that this place, this nexus, was built solely for them, but also from them." Bakli's voice was soft, a series of little chirps. "He is building his energies. They need to create their homes. Cosmo was closest in the making of his nest. When the building is done, then the babies will come. Make this home yours *and* his. That is when the babies will come." Bakli smiled at him. "I cannot wait for the babies to come. We love babies."

"I do too." He'd never imagined—well, he had, but not in an actual physical way—that there would be babies.

And now with this knowledge, he felt as if he could breathe.

If they never had children, it wouldn't matter to him, but it did to Cosmo.

And so they would finish their explorations of the house and create a glorious home together.

Suddenly, something that Bakli said pinged in his brain. "You said other worlds. There is the human world, Lunastra, the Land of Summer. Are there others?"

Bakli gave him a pursed lip and the most adorable little frown ever. "Why in the universe would there only be three? Those are the strongest openings, but they are not alone."

"Oh, that could complicate things." He chewed on his bottom lip. Hopefully, they'd be able to communicate. "Well, I suppose we will search for them. Look for them, protect them. Oh dear…"

"The magic will provide." Bakli's laugh was merry. "For now, work on your house and your family. This core family will be together for a very long time, and this place In Between will become a warren of joy. Allow yourself to experience it." He frowned deeply. "And no more napping!"

"How about small naps?"

"Small naps are fine, no more than a month."

His laugh huffed out, happy and deep, almost knocking Bakli down. "Oh, you absolutely have my word."

He wasn't sure his Cosmo could go an entire month without anything.

Maybe without sleep?

That he could imagine.

But why would he sleep so long now? He had his mate to keep him busy as well. He loved Cosmo so.

"Now, about my hoard…"

FOURTEEN

Cosmo helped Cullen move a chest of drawers into his bedroom. They'd found it in Hawk's attic, which was full of the most amazing shit, and Cullen had immediately claimed it as his. It was huge, and he was panting by the time they got it into place.

"Why didn't we make Corbin and Hawk move this?" Cosmo asked.

"Because Corbin would have called it for his seed collection."

"Oh, good point." Cullen's house was fascinating. It was a massive A-frame, formed from huge logs, or what seemed like massive beams, but something had happened, and the house had hundreds of secret doors and hidden places to wander, tunnels to explore. It was a marvelous place—not scary, just fun.

And somehow, no matter how often any of them wandered, no matter where they went, they ended up back at the big kitchen that formed the rear of Hawk and Corbin's house.

"I think it looks perfect here, don't you? What are you going to put in it?"

"Toys. I think it would be so much fun to have a place with a ton of toys." Cullen patted the dresser, bouncing. "I want this to be a game room."

"That's cool, I like that. Put the dangerous ones at the top, hmm?" One day, there would be babies. One day, these houses would be filled with family.

"Yes. We put them in order of age. Crawling, toddling, and then the adult toys all the way up at the top."

"Good deal." He helped get the piece in just the right place, then stepped back to watch.

Oh, it was perfect. It fit just right.

And Cullen was making it this...colorful, wonderful place full of pillows and blankets and illusions. He could get lost in there for days.

"Perfect. Now help me move my bed to that wall."

Cosmo groaned. "Your bed is a wall. Why don't you have slider thingies to move it?"

"I do." Cullen beamed, holding up an Amazon package.

"Oh, good deal." That would make it way easier. They got the ends lifted a tiny bit and the gliders placed underneath, and it was like whoosh. The bed was moved in seconds.

They grabbed each other's hands and bounced up on it, flopping hard.

"Man, I want a milkshake," Cullen said.

"Well, we just happen to have ice cream."

"In a minute." He looked at the chest from across the room.

The curtains blew, the featherlight fabric brushing against the bureau.

It was amazing to him because, if you looked out the

window that was next to the furniture, the light poured in and it was summertime, puffy clouds lolling across the sky.

There were roses blooming, and the trees were deep green and full. And if you looked just right, you could see his mother's house up on the top of the hill, the curved shape almost hidden by a multitude of roses. He could smell them, along with apple and honey. It was pure warmth.

If he'd looked out the window in Corbin's house just now, it was springtime. Flowers and trees were just beginning to bud. Everything was light green and...actually, they were kind of the color of Corbin. Everything was beginning to grow and sprout and be beautiful.

This morning, from the windows in their house, it was the deepest part of autumn. It was that moment, right before the snows came, when everything had gone quiet.

Harvest was over and there was this deep waiting silence, like the world was whispering, 'go to bed, go to bed, go to bed.'

Even better, it was pouring outside of Corbin's windows, and there may be snow tomorrow in his. Here, there was a summer squall, just begging to water the flowers.

So much fun.

"It's cool, huh?"

Cosmo nodded to his brother. "Yes, but I have to admit I don't miss the constant summer, and I'm ready for fall—I want our Halloween party. Of course, we're lucky. If we get tired of one season, we can go somewhere else."

"I know! There's something exciting about scary stories and casseroles and harvest festivals. In Lunastra, it's all asparagus and eggs."

"I know. It's wild and wonderful, all at the same time."

He grinned at Cullen, tickled. This felt so normal. "What kind of toys?"

"Well, I think games, puzzles. Books. Things that will last. Because. I mean, this is our home. We're going to be here. We might as well be prepared to stay and enjoy ourselves. Also cards. I love cards." Cullen rubbed his fingers together and a slew of cards seemed to fly at Cosmo, spin around him like wild black and red butterflies. And then they flew away back into his hands before they disappeared.

Cosmo applauded. "You've been practicing."

"It's so much easier here. I imagine it's because I don't have to worry about covering us up, about us having different skin or eyes or anything. I can just spend all the magic making things. I know they're not real, but they're so much fun."

"Show me your best thing." He leaned against the windowsill, the scent of rain getting stronger.

"Okay, I've been working on this. Stand back."

Wait for me! Corbin's call came from deep within the house. *I want to see too.*

Well then, come on. I'm going to make it happen soon. I've been working hard. They chuckled as Corbin came barreling in, screeching to a halt just in time to slam right into him. Both of them rocking together and tangling in the curtains.

Did I make it?

You made it.

"Okay, we're going to have to focus. Are you ready?"

"We're ready."

Cullen closed his eyes and rubbed his hands together. At first, he moved them up and down, and then began to drag them in circles over and over and over again.

The horse appeared first, beautiful and white. Then a tail appeared, blowing in a soft breeze.

Oh, it's lovely.

He's not done.

I don't think he's done this before.

Not yet, Corbin.

Cullen made a tube with his hands clasped together and a column of smoke appeared, then he drew his hands up, tightening them slowly all the while. It was as if Cullen had formed a cone.

Then Cullen put the cone on the horse's forehead, and it became a twisted, beautiful silver spiral. The perfect horn.

The big head turned to look at him, those dark eyes, so blue and so perfect. The fur so white it glowed.

"You made a unicorn!"

"It looks good, doesn't it?"

"He's just gorgeous."

"I'm so proud."

Cullen bowed. "Thank you."

"I like the room, too, Bro." Corbin looked out the window as the unicorn leaped out and galloped across the yard. "And the view is stellar."

"It is. I think I want a milkshake."

Cosmo grinned at Corbin, who rolled his eyes. "Well, we just happen to have ice cream."

The unicorn whinnied, the sound solid and incredibly real, and Corbin leaned out the window to see. "That's impressive, bud."

"Yeah, you don't usually—"

Cullen blinked. "It's not me."

"What?"

"I didn't do it. It's not me. I mean I made the illusion, but not the real thing..."

"Well, at least it went the right way." Cosmo wasn't going to freak out. Who really knew what went on out there in the Land of Summer, which was where Cullen's house faced.

"That was new," Corbin murmured.

"We all focused like he told us. Maybe we did it together."

Cullen looked a little wild around the eyes. "Let's go make milkshakes. I can come back and move furniture in a bit."

Food was always the answer when they were wigged out.

"Good idea." Corbin led the way back out of Cullen's bedroom, heading down to the communal area that kept... changing to suit them. It was mostly Hawk's kitchen and dining room, but then the great room seemed to be from... He didn't know. Maybe Myk's brothers' house? Or maybe it was a manifestation they'd made too.

Whatever. It was comfy.

It was really weird how everything had changed so much, so quickly.

Everything for the dragons was new, but only for them. The ways that the houses had altered and shifted seemed to be stabilized in the dragon world.

Here it was less so. Here, the house was in constant flux.

Cosmo supposed that made sense because they were living in between at least three great big worlds.

He sighed.

He was really tired of having to think all the time.

Maybe he should just appreciate it. The space was glorious. A weird amalgamation of three different homes and the three of them plus Hawk—it was a warm, cozy, comfortable space with books and puzzles and places to be together.

That's what this was. It was their place to be together while still having homes that were separate.

He blinked and looked at his brothers. "You do realize that this is the best house?"

Corbin tilted his head. "Well, there's three houses."

Cullen chuckled. "And one house. Like us."

"One house, one heartbeat, three bodies."

They started to laugh, all three of them just cracking up.

It was perfect. They lived in the perfect house, and he hadn't even noticed that until right now. He'd been so involved in the grumpiness of having to worry and deal with the cleaning and the organizing and the moving and the...

But the house was helping, this space was good, and they were so lucky.

"What's funny?" *Can I come in? Would I be disturbing you?* That voice belonged to Hawk.

Come. You're always welcome with us. Always.

Hawk wandered in, covered in dust and cobwebs, and the three of them stopped and stared.

"What happened?"

"I was exploring," Hawk explained.

"Did you take water?"

"And a snack."

"And did you leave a note?"

Their questions flashed out one right after the other. There were rules for a reason. They didn't have a lot of rules, but those rules they did have were important.

"I, uh..."

"Hawk," he admonished.

"I'm sorry. I'll remember next time."

"You're forgiven," Corbin said. "Did you find anything amazing?"

"I found my hoard." Hawk beamed. "I had a little help."

Cosmo tilted his head. "From who?"

"Bakli, would you care to meet my mate?"

A tiny man appeared out of a little door that opened in the kitchen wall. "Hello. I am Bakli."

Cosmo gaped. The guy looked like a Christmas elf from an old cartoon. "Hello, Bakli. I'm Cosmo. And this is Corbin and Cullen." They all bowed to the little man. "We were about to make milkshakes. Would you like some ice cream?"

Bakli reached into his hat and produced a mug the size of a thimble. "That would be welcomed."

He was not going to giggle. Nope. Not even close. But that was the cutest thing ever.

"I'll get making," Cullen said, grinning.

"Thank you." Bakli let Hawk lift him up to sit on the table, where he sat tailor style, nodding to all of them.

"Did Bakli help you find your hoard, love?" Cosmo asked.

"He did. He says he's been here waiting for me to return, and for the house to fill with you and your brothers." Hawk gave Bakli a warm smile.

"So you knew Hawk before?"

"Oh, yes. It was a bit disconcerting when the house came but Hawk stayed asleep elsewhere." Bakli patted Hawk's hand. "It is good to see him."

"Thank you, friend. I'm overjoyed to be home with my mate." Hawk drew Cosmo in, hugging him tight.

"I am glad."

"So, does anyone want chocolate syrup?" Cullen asked. "Or do we want fruit?"

"I like cherry," Cosmo said, raising an eyebrow at Hawk. "I also like cherry fruit."

"Sounds good," Corbin said. "Bakli?"

"Oh yes. I very much like fruit."

"Perfect! Fruit it is."

"So, Bakli, it's so nice to meet you." He hadn't even known there were house spirits to meet.

Bakli smiled at him. "It is also nice to meet you and to be able to come out and about. We weren't sure if you were amenable to having non-dragons in the house."

Cosmo winked at Bakli. "Well, we're only half dragon, and we're totally welcoming. Do you have a large family?"

"Yes, there is my husband and I, and we have seven children."

"Oh my!" Seven? As in one less than eight. "That is a blessing worth of children."

They were going to have to get toys for the children. After they found out how old they were, of course, but also how big, because that must be very small.

He would figure it out. They were smart dragons.

"It is a grand lot of children, but they are all good children. They are learning to help us with our jobs."

"What jobs do you have?"

"We work for the home."

Cosmo tilted his head a little confused, but more curious. "For the home? So you work for Hawk?"

"No. No. Mr. Hawk is our friend."

They stared at each other, obviously confused.

Hawk cleared his throat. "I believe what Bakli means is that he works for the house. This is his house and our house, and together, we work to keep the place functioning. He helps in so many different ways, things that we rarely even notice."

"Oh, I see, I understand." He didn't, but he thought maybe he did.

It was much like Tyson's Helena or Ob and Bob. House spirits took many forms, and he was just incredibly grateful that his house spirit liked milkshakes and wasn't pissed off.

Cullen perked up. "Does my house have house spirits? I want to meet my house spirits! They don't even have to do anything. I just want to talk to them and see if they can show me anything else in the house. I'm working very hard on making tricks."

Bakli shook his head. "I don't have access to the other parts of the houses. This is my house."

Cosmo frowned. "But this is the common area. This is all the houses."

"Yes, and this is my door to that."

"Okay. Well, I hope you're happy. Is there anything that we can do for you that we're not doing yet?"

Bakli tilted his head. "We very much like milk."

"Ah, yes." Hawk smiled. "We will get some for you, my friend. My memory can be foggy, so I didn't get any on the way here."

So he'd ask Hawk what portions of milk to serve to the… little people. He wondered what Bakli's people called themselves.

Nisse, love. They're nisse.

Oh, cool. Thanks. He beamed at Hawk.

"Do you have house spirits, Corbin?" Cullen asked.

Corbin shrugged. "If I do, I haven't seen them. I worry that the…the problems ran them off."

"So what do we do to let them know, if we have them, that they're welcome to come say hi?" Cullen asked, looking at Bakli.

Bakli beamed. "Excellent question! Make your homes

your own, your havens, your nests. The happy spirits will return and be awake."

That made Cullen smile and nod, as if a question had been answered, but Corbin's expression still looked troubled, and Cosmo moved over across the kitchen to help with the milkshakes.

What is it? What's wrong?

Corbin shook his head, lips tight. *What if I can't.*

What if you can't what?

What if I can't fix it? This. Corbin's hands shook as he worked. *My gift is making something grow. This is blood. This dragon blood is in the boards, it's deep in the fibers, and it hurts. What if I can't remove it and make things right?*

Then we raze it.

Pure shock was written across Corbin's face. *What?*

If we can't clean it, then we take it out. We remove it. And we burn it.

The thought came as clear as crystal slamming into his brain.

Corbin blinked. *Can we do that?*

Why not?

What would Myk say?

Why would Myk have to know? He can't come in here. He can't leave the veil. You and I? We're the only ones who would know. Cullen. Hawk. Who are we going to tell? We take it out and we remove it. No one ever knows. We're the ones who live here. This is our home. We fix it.

As easy as that.

He shrugged one shoulder. *Doesn't matter if it's easy or not. It is what it is. This is your home. Your life. We're stuck here in this place. No, we were chosen to be here in this place, and I'm going to make it mine, and you're going to make it yours. Fuck anybody who says otherwise.*

Tension seemed to drain out of Corbin. Then he nodded, pouring the milkshakes into glasses. *Right. All right, yes, I can do that. We can do that.* Corbin gave him a warm grin, and his elder brother seemed to stand up a little bit taller. *Thank you, brother.*

I love you.

Corbin began to pass out glasses, and Hawk came back up to Cosmo, one arm around his waist.

You did well.

It seemed like the right thing to do.

It was perfect. Hawk's smile was blinding. *Absolutely perfect.*

Feeling like a million dollars, like he had turned a corner in a road he hadn't realized he was walking on, Cosmo lifted his glass. "To us."

And everyone else lifted their mugs as well.

"Cheers."

FIFTEEN

Something had changed in Cosmo. Hawk could see it. It was as if someone had turned on a light that had been dimmed since Hawk had known him.

It wasn't just Cosmo though. It was all three of them. Something inside of them had eased. Had lightened.

Hawk was over the moon.

He heard his sweet rosy dragon whistling. And the sound of something moving, deep inside the house.

Curious, he started wandering, searching room by room. He had a basic idea of where Cosmo was, somewhere in the center of the house, in one of the rooms that was smaller and not often used. Something dusty and dark.

No, not dark. Cozy.

Hawk had noticed that Cosmo was trying to use more positive language. It was cute as hell. Cozy.

BANG!

Cosmo?

"Mate?"

Oh dear. That wasn't mental. That was vocal, which

was probably bad, because that meant that Cosmo didn't want him to really know what was going on.

"Are you okay?"

"Oh yeah, I'm fine. I was just. Moving something... heavy."

He'd obviously done enough searching, and so he found Cosmo with his mind. He simply went straight to Cosmo, finding him smack dab in the center of the house.

Literally in the heart of the house.

This was a room with no windows and precious little but a chair, a bookshelf, and stairs—one going up and one going down. It functioned more as a landing than a room really. And yet, somehow, Cosmo had managed to drag up a desk, or possibly a dresser. It was an odd piece of...

"What is that and how did you get it up here?" Hawk asked.

"I dragged it. It's a map case."

"Oh. Do you have many maps?"

"No, but I like it. Do you like it?" Cosmo gave him a hopeful smile.

"I—"

"I ordered it online, it came today."

"Ah." He didn't really know what to say. Cosmo was perfectly within his rights to bring a map case up to this room. "Do you need help?"

Cosmo blinked at him a little bit and then smiled. "I would love some. Can you help me move it over here to this corner? I thought it would be a good place for a lamp. Then I thought you could put some of your more special pieces from your hoard in the drawers so that they'd be safe, and you could look at them without getting so dusty."

Hawk melted. "You bought this for me?"

"I did. I thought this is a safe place. No one knows really

that this room is here, and then you would have a place where you could sit with a lamp and look at your favorite stones."

Hawk grabbed Cosmo up and kissed him hard. "I love it. Thank you."

Cosmo gave him a wicked grin. "How much do you love it?"

"Very much, my love." Hawk tugged Cosmo against him. "In fact, I want to show you how much. But not here where it's still so dusty."

Cosmo kissed him again, moaning, which surprised him. This was escalating quickly.

"Let's go to our room." Cosmo took his hand and pulled him, racing with him in far better than human speed to their room, where he started stripping off Hawk's clothing. He was flushed brighter than usual, and his fingers trembled. "Need you."

Hawk smiled slowly, taking in Cosmo's scent and feeling something click into place that hadn't before.

Cosmo was in heat, he thought.

"Anything you need, my love." He pressed Cosmo down on the bed, his cock rising, readying his knot to do what it was meant for. He took a kiss that had Cosmo writhing and yanking at Hawk's clothes.

"Promise?" Cosmo said, gaze begging him to help him.

"Yes, my love, I promise. Anything at all."

Cosmo stretched, curling his fingers and toes, really going with it.

He'd been in bed. For days. Like three days, he thought, but he'd sort of lost track. He'd sent Hawk down to the kitchen for food and beverage, and now he was just waiting to see what Hawk had scrounged.

Cosmo sat up, pulling the sheet around his waist to remove temptation when Hawk came back. They couldn't seem to keep their hands off each other.

He supposed it was normal. After all, the houses—well, it'd never been bad, but it was coming together nicely now. Cosmo felt that everything, not just the bedroom, had little touches that belonged to him too.

There were dozens of little places to sit and snuggle. To read. To play games. Just to talk.

Goddess knew he loved to sit and chat for hours over a jigsaw puzzle, a game of Go or chess.

Cosmo snuggled back into the pillows, glancing out the window. The snow had started around mid-October, and now that they were sliding into Thanksgiving, everything was deep and white.

Most of their supplies had been brought in already. They could get down to pick up packages if they needed to, but it was dangerous to fly there, so they tried to only do it once a month.

Fortunately for them, if they needed fresh veggies, they could just pop out to the dragon side of the universe where it was, happily, summer. They could get ripe berries, lettuce, and whatever they needed that was tasty and good. It was really handy how that worked out.

Hawk was very into making smoothies, especially out of some of the fruits that were unusual to him.

As if thinking of Hawk made him appear, his mate walked in, smoothies and a massive plate of sandwiches in his hand.

He arched one eyebrow at the stack of sandwiches, and

Hawk shrugged. "Your brothers have been worried about us. They sent sandwiches."

"I like sandwiches and I'm starving." He wiggled happily, his stomach snarling. "The snow's coming down again."

"It is. I love it. It reminds me of when I was young." Hawk tilted his head. "I think it does, at any rate."

"Tell me about it?"

"There was lots of snow. But also volcanic stuff underground. So hot springs. Hot sand. All the good stuff. I would have to ask Bakli exactly where it was…"

Hawk came to sit with him, the sandwiches between them, handing him a smoothie.

"Thank you, love." He grinned because he would probably rather have hot chocolate, but Hawk was so proud of his blender skills.

"You're welcome. And Corbin said hot chocolate and cookies downstairs tonight. We are not just invited, we are required."

Cosmo laughed softly. "That sounds like Corbin."

"I am not offended." He grabbed a sandwich.

"What kind do we have?"

"Ham and cheese. Turkey and provolone. I think tuna fish."

He gagged a little bit. "No tuna. No, I think turkey and provolone for me, thank you." That actually sounded really yummy. "So, cocoa, huh? Are we having a movie night? Did he say?"

Corbin had decided that they were having family night at least once a week. Sometimes they played games, sometimes they did puzzles, sometimes they watched movies, sometimes they kicked each other's asses on Fortnite.

It just depended.

It was kind of unfair how good Hawk was at video games, considering he'd never even seen one before they had met. Whatever.

That part didn't matter.

The part that mattered was all of them together, bundled up on the great big couch, being idiots together.

He knew what was important.

Hawk grabbed his smoothie and handed Cosmo a quarter of a turkey sandwich before settling on the bed and arranging himself. "How are you, mate? Are you sore?"

"Oh, you'd like that, wouldn't you? That would make you feel all alpha dragon studly. 'I knotted my mate twenty-seven thousand times in the last three days. Are you tender?'"

Hawk grinned, totally unrepentant. "Uh-huh. So are you sore?"

"Yeah, in that don't touch it, it's tired sort of way." Cosmo cracked up. "I'm fairly sure that a couple of the times we did that, I could taste you when I swallowed."

They both started laughing, just kind of howling their joy. The simple fact was they had been together and had really had an enormous amount of fun. In fact, Cosmo was thinking that he might be done with fun for at least, oh, five or six hours now.

Hawk grabbed him and hugged him tight. "Have I mentioned how incredibly joyful I am that you were in my home when I got here?"

Cosmo snorted, tossing his head. "I am your home, dragon. Also? I need to wash my hair."

Hawk nodded. "We'll bathe after we eat, and I'll wash everything. Make sure it's all clean."

"You'll wash gently—everything right?"

That started them laughing again.

"Absolutely everything." Hawk winked for him, then tore into a sandwich. He seemed ravenous.

Cosmo got that actually. His sammy and smoothie were gone so fast that he blinked at the empty glass in his hand. Huh.

He set the glass aside and took up another sandwich piece. "These are yummy." He peered at it to make sure it wasn't tuna.

"They are. I wish there were chips. I should have thought of chips."

He laughed at Hawk's lament. "I could ask Cullen to bring them up."

"Mmm. No. Not just now. I want you all to myself for just a bit longer."

"To snuggle but nothing else, right?" He wasn't up to anything else. In fact, he was starting to get sleepy again halfway through this sandwich.

"Yes. You look tired, love." Hawk reached out to stroke his cheek.

"I am, kinda. Is that weird?"

"No. I think we should curl up together. If I do not wish to sleep, I will read."

"Oh, I like that."

He did too. He loved the idea of just snuggling up and resting. He wasn't hiding. Wasn't worried or nesting or... anything.

He was just happy.

It worked for him.

He liked it a lot. Cosmo yawned, putting the plate of sandwiches on the little table that sat far enough away that he wouldn't smell tuna. It was a reach, but he didn't want it on the bedside table.

Hawk reeled him back in when he leaned too far.

CHAPTER

SIXTEEN

Hawk watched Cosmo dance around the kitchen with Corbin, the waltz getting to the point where it needed to sweep out to the dining room, or cookies were going to start flying…

There was something different about him. Something Hawk couldn't put a finger on. A glow, he thought. It seemed to light his Rose from within, making his pink skin shine, making his eyes light up.

Who knew? Hawk felt as though he was glowing half the time now. He was polished and loved and admired on a regular basis. His scales gleamed. And he was… present. Every day.

He wasn't just slogging through time, waiting for sleep to take him again so he could hide. He had pride in his life again.

He was a guardian of at least three realms. Maybe more.

Cullen plopped down next to him. "Not dancing?"

"No, they wanted to dance together. What about you?"

"Not a dancer. I like to sing though. I'm more of an

entertainer." Cullen clapped his hands together and flower petals sprayed everywhere. "It's a gift."

"It's a pretty cool gift." Cullen was getting really good at making complicated shapes, not just fast-flying things. Although you did have to watch the little dragon. When they were playing games, he could invent new pieces and hold them just long enough for him to convince them they were doing something wrong. "How's your house going?"

"Good. I've decided to create it like a giant escape room where I know all the answers to all the riddles."

"Okay, that's fair." A little strange, but he knew he had a sort of hidden super hoard room. So he really couldn't judge.

"Do you think that Cosmo's pregnant?"

"What?"

"Cosmo, the pink one. You know him, right? You've been like doing the—" Cullen stuck his index finger through the ring that his thumb and his other index finger made, and performed a definitive, penetrative act motion.

"Yes, Cullen, I know who he is. And yes. We've been intimate."

"Oh, fancy. I guess that's better than just fucking. Still, that wasn't my question. Do you think he is with child? Knocked up? Preggers? Cooking a bun in the oven? Hatching an egg?"

"Well, he hasn't said anything, and he hasn't been throwing up in the mornings..."

"You know that that's not, like, absolutely necessary. Some people don't."

"Honestly, the number of dragons I've known that have been pregnant I can count on one hand," Hawk admitted.

"We need at least two, possibly also a foot. And you

don't have to have morning sickness. But he looks different. He seems different."

"Maybe he's simply happy."

"Does happy make you smell different? I mean, I guess it could. I don't think so, though. We've been happy and unhappy a bunch. I don't remember ever being like 'Oh, you stink with unhappiness. Hmm, you smell like roses. You must be so happy'."

Hawk stopped and stared at him. "You think he smells like roses?"

Hawk had always thought Cosmo smelled like roses, but the boys had always suggested that he was insane.

"Yeah, kind of. Kind of a lot like roses."

"Hmmm." Hawk pondered that. "I suppose we'll know soon enough if he is." Their several-day binge on each other had rather seemed like heat sex.

"That would be cool. To have a baby around. It's so not fair you can't go to Lunastra."

"Mmm." Hawk had learned to keep his noises noncommittal when it came to the dragonlands. It was a moot point. If he went through, he couldn't come back. So he stayed where he was.

"Yeah, I know. I've talked to Cosmo about it." Cullen gave him a quick little glance. "I think it's cool that you're not being a bitch about this whole thing, you know. I think it's... I mean we're triplets. We need each other, and he needs you. And that makes you family."

"Thank you, Cullen. I'm honored to be your family."

"I wish you could meet the boss though. You'd like him. You two would get along great."

He still couldn't believe that his Cosmo had been part of some sort of strange rescue team. It seemed to him that Cosmo was this sweet, gentle, innocent omega, and he just… He simply couldn't see it. He simply couldn't see Cosmo and the others out there rescuing dragons.

Part of him wondered if perhaps he had somehow misunderstood what they said they did. But he didn't know.

He just couldn't see it.

"Yeah. Ah well." Cullen waved a hand. "Anyway. Cosmo. Preggers."

"I'll just ask him how he feels," Hawk murmured.

"Oh, cool. That way we don't have to."

Hawk chuckled, watching Corbin dip Cosmo in a most dramatic way. "No. That will be my job."

"Coolios." Cullen surprised him with a kiss to his cheek. "You want a cookie?"

"Hmm. Yes. I would love a white chocolate one with the nuts."

"Those are the best! Want to play Yahtzee?" Cullen got up to grab cookies, even as Corbin and Cosmo said—

"Ooh! Yahtzee!"

"I like Yahtzee." Dice games he understood. Some of the cooperative games the trips owned baffled him. How did anyone win?

But Yahtzee was like an ancient game he remembered. And it was fun.

He would pour drinks.

Something was wrong with Hawk.

Cosmo didn't know what, but there was something off. His mate was treating him like…

Like he was a piece of porcelain, like he was breakable,

which he wasn't. He was strong, and he could fight. He knew how.

He came off a little dip-shitty because he really could. He was in a safe space with his brothers, and he didn't have to be all *grr argh* serious.

He could just be... Cosmo.

But that didn't mean that Hawk had permission to treat him like he was fragile. He was not fragile. It had been happening all evening too.

Through Yahtzee and Clue and a backgammon tournament, which had been kind of fierce. Corbin had won, of course. Jerk.

No, it was late, like the wee hours in the morning late, and he was sleepy.

They were getting ready for bed, Hawk stealing these weird little glances at him.

"What's wrong?" Cosmo finally asked.

"What?" Hawk tried for innocent, but he was shitty at it. He was way too old...

"Don't be weird. Something's wrong. I can tell. You keep looking at me like I'm a bug or something."

Hawk gasped, hand literally going to his heart. "I do not."

"You totally do. Like you're utterly giving me bug-looking vibes. What's the matter?"

Whatever it was, it would be fine. Cosmo knew it in his bones. They could fix it. So Hawk just needed to come out with it.

"Are you pregnant?" Hawk asked.

Okay. That hadn't been on his radar of things he needed to worry about today. "Well, I don't think so. I don't know, but I haven't thrown up yet. Isn't throwing up part of it?"

"Apparently Cullen says that no, throwing up does not necessarily have to be part of it."

"Oh, because Cullen's an expert. At any rate, I don't know. I mean it's not like we take dragon pregnancy tests. Maybe if they have some for lizards or big birds." That might work in a clinical setting.

Hawk glared at him. "I think you're supposed to know. Like. Can you feel them? Anything inside there like? Magic."

"Everything feels like magic, Hawk."

Hawk pursed his lips. "Well, I suppose you are made of two magical beings and so that would make sense. What does it feel like? Does the magic feel any different?"

"Not really. How did you know to ask?" That seemed to be an important question. His eyebrows lowered. "Not Corbin."

"Corbin. No, it was totally Cullen."

"But Corbin's the one who grows things."

Hawk shrugged. "I know. No, it was Cullen. He says you're more pink than normal."

"Huh. Maybe I should contact my mother?" Mom probably had a few things to say.

"Are you sure you'll be able to get back in if you leave?" Hawk's brows drew down in concern.

"Oh yeah. We don't have a problem going any of the directions. I've been to see Mom a few times, but it would be even better if she could come here and meet you."

"That doesn't seem fair."

He gave Hawk an arch glare. "Nobody ever said life was fair, and she can only come when it's like a direct descendant."

"Honestly?"

"That's what it seems to be, but who knows?" The fae had way more rules.

"Hmm. It would be interesting to meet more of your family. I am not opposed to meeting her at all. So I suppose if she will come here, then that would be lovely."

"I'll send word then."

Just like that. Boom. It didn't have to be difficult. Unless...

"You really are kinda wigged out by the idea, huh? When did your moms... um, leave?" Hawk never talked about his family, so Cosmo was curious.

"Oh, many years ago. So many I've lost count." He could feel Hawk try to picture his mothers, and they were a fuzzy, distant memory.

Goddess, that was...

"Hawk." Cosmo moved to lay a hand on Hawk's arm. "Are you going to be super disappointed if we aren't pregnant?"

Hawk stared at him. "I admit, I've had many sweet thoughts about what our baby might look like. A mix of you and me. That would be fun." Hawk chuckled. "But you know very well I can live without it. We've discussed this."

"We have. I just wanted to make sure you hadn't changed your mind."

Hawk blinked at Cosmo. "Of course not. I love you so much." Hawk reached for him, pulling him close, those lips hovering above his. "No matter what happens, you have that."

"I do." And that he felt inside him. Like the magic Hawk was talking about. "I love you too."

Hawk nodded. "Then that is all I need."

"Cool." He twined his arms around Hawk's neck. "That means you'll stop treating me like I'm made of glass? I want you."

Hawk's gaze heated, his eyes glowing gold for a moment. "No more glass."

"Now that," Cosmo said between kisses, "is what I want to hear."

SEVENTEEN

Hawk straightened his shirt, which somehow had manifested this morning as sort of a lovely embroidered tunic. The pants were a matching leather, which he hadn't worn in a few centuries, he was certain, and he had high boots on as well.

He was dressed to meet Cosmo's mother.

No one had told him to expect her today, but apparently, his closet knew things he didn't.

Even the colors were his old family livery, the red and gold and black impossible to miss.

He brushed his hands down his chest and belly, then took a deep breath. Yes, all right. All he could do to prepare, he had done. So Hawk wandered down to the kitchen, ready to face whatever judgment Cosmo's mother had for him.

"Wow, you look nice today, Hawk." Corbin blinked at him from the kitchen table, where he sat nursing a cup of coffee. Corbin wore pajamas printed with polar bears wearing hats and scarves.

"You are also sartorially pleasant this morning," Hawk said.

"Thanks. I get these every holiday from Tyson."

"He's of the Estes clutch?"

"Mmmhmm. So why are you all..." Corbin flapped a hand. "Dressed."

"Your mother is coming."

"No shit?" Corbin immediately rose and began cleaning the kitchen.

"Can I help?"

"No, just stay there and be clean. Goddess, why is Mother coming?" Corbin actually sounded worried.

"Is she unkind?"

"Depends on who you're talking to on whether she's unkind or not. My brothers, no. Never."

Oh dear. "She's coming to speak to Cosmo."

"She's coming to tell him he's pregnant." Corbin's voice was dry as dust.

"Well, I hope so."

"I bet you do." Corbin looked over his shoulder at him and grinned. "So do I. I mean, not about the Mom coming part, but about the baby part. I'm into growing things."

So why hadn't Cosmo told him that Corbin and his mother had a problem? It seemed relatively important. *Mate.*

Hmm? What do you need?

I just told Corbin that your mother is coming to see you.

Okay.

Do you have anything you need to tell me?

Uh. I'm wearing white, so whatever we do for breakfast, it shouldn't be messy.

Cosmo! Oh, he loved his mate, but damn, Cosmo was so frustrating.

What?

Why is Corbin panicking?

Ah, it's just Corbin. The thought was utterly dismissive. *He gets weird.*

This seems larger than weird, mate.

No, it's just that his magic and her magic are the same magic, and that makes them all angry all the time about each other. It's never ugly; it's always been this way. It's sort of the same thing if you said that our dad was coming. Cullen and I would be a little concerned, but he can't, so we don't have to worry about it.

Oh.

Well, that was interesting. He did understand that oftentimes when dragons were very, very similar there were conflicts. It did seem incredibly unfair to poor Corbin that the only parent who could come and visit was the one that he didn't particularly get along with.

But Hawk was going to be very quietly pleased that it wasn't Cosmo. Very quietly.

He started drying dishes and putting them away, and Corbin offered him a friendly, if slightly worried, smile.

"So tell me about your mother."

"She's fae. She's very persnickety. She does like things the way that she likes them, and she loves roses. Flowers. All flowers of any kind, in fact. She believes that vegetables are a waste of flower space."

"Well, I for one am grateful for your vegetable garden, and for the greenhouse. It's so nice to have fresh vegetables."

Corbin rolled his eyes, but he did smile. "Thanks, brother. I know it's unreasonable, isn't it? She just gets under my skin. I could never grow anything the right way. If she could go outside and see the roses out here in the front of the house, she would tell me they were too antique or not red enough. Possibly the thorns were too long or not curved correctly. Perhaps the vine should spell out 'I love my mother'. That sort of thing."

"Oh, how fun, though. If you could spell things with vines." The thought charmed him.

"It's easier with ivy. It just doesn't grow as well here. Roses do so much better with the soil."

"Ah. Yes. The acidic soil of the desert is their natural milieu." He sighed. "I didn't mean to make trouble, brother."

"Bah." Corbin came to give him an unexpected hug, and one he accepted with true gladness. The familial feeling he got from being with Cosmo's brothers grew every day.

Much like Corbin's flowers.

"It's no trouble. She will say what she says, and I will rebut, and all will be well."

"Mmm. What can we have for breakfast that will not be messy?"

"Hot Pockets."

"Hot what?" His eyebrows went up.

"Hot Pockets—you know, pastry with goo?" Corbin waggled his eyebrows.

"I have no idea what you mean. Well, I have had pastry with goo. Mostly in Paris or Rome."

"Yeah, this is not that." Corbin chuckled. "But they're fun, and not too messy."

"Hmmm."

"And they come in bacon and egg. What are you cleaning for, Corbin?" Cullen bounced in and went right to the coffeepot.

"Mother."

"Oh, that's why there are so many more flowers outside

my door. Cool. Maybe she'll bring up some of those wild orange mushrooms. Those make for magic illusions..."

Corbin rolled his eyes and fought his grin. "You do know they're poisonous, right?"

"Only if you eat them!" Cullen singsonged.

Hawk blinked at them. "You eat poisonous things?" That seemed silly. Why on earth would anyone do that?

Cosmo came down to the kitchen, and he was wearing a lovely loose tunic and a pair of pants in solid white. He glowed against it, his rose-colored skin so bright, his scales showing. Time in the sandpit was doing wonders for him.

"You know you don't have to clean for mother."

Corbin fastened a glare on his brother. "You know *you* don't have to clean for mother."

Cosmo rolled his eyes. "Corbin has issues. Mommy issues."

"You know if I shove you out the door of Cullen's house and lock it, Hawk can't go out there and save you."

Cosmo pursed his lips. "You wouldn't."

"Try me. You're the one who invited Mother here without asking. You know the rules. You have to at least warn me."

"There's no need to be a panicky idiot. She loves you."

Corbin crossed his arms, tilted his head, and lifted one eyebrow. "I'm sure she loves fruit too, before she bites into it and then devours it whole!"

Hawk was beginning to think that perhaps he'd made a terrible mistake.

Cullen chuckled. "It's fine, Hawk. They just had a big fight the last time they saw each other. It was ridiculous."

Corbin opened his mouth, and Cullen gave him a long-suffering look.

"Oh come on, you guys were arguing about poop."

"Fertilizer."

"Poop."

"Whatever!" Cosmo actually stomped his foot. "Anytime you disagree about the slightest little thing, it becomes this big ordeal."

Then Corbin got a hurt look on his face that broke Hawk's heart a little bit. "You guys always take her side. I never take anybody's side over yours. You always take her side."

Cosmo shook his head. "I swear, we didn't even get into this one. We weren't even there. I only said that I didn't care."

"That would be because we don't care," Cullen pointed out. "It's poop."

"Fertilizer!" Corbin hollered, and Cosmo went right to Corbin.

Hawk was afraid for a moment that Cosmo was going to hit Corbin in the nose. He'd seen a couple of the triplet fights, and they were never as entertaining or pleasant as his fantasies led him to believe they might be. But Cosmo just hugged his brother tight.

"I'm sorry we didn't tell you. I just need to know if I'm pregnant. I don't have any of the grossness. There's supposed to be grossness. Barfing and stuff."

"Are you complaining?" Corbin asked, and Cosmo shrugged.

"Only because I want it to be normal, the baby, everything. But that's all, and I'm sorry."

To Corbin's credit, he immediately accepted the apology and squeezed his brother back. "I hope that you're pregnant and that it's normal too. I am going to be the best uncle ever."

Cullen rolled his eyes. "Unlikely. I'm gonna be the fun

one. You're going to be the weird one who ends up giving him, like, medicine and making him eat his broccoli. I can make things appear."

"Talk to me when you're hungry, Butthead."

"I am now. Can we have Hot Pockets?"

Hawk nodded, pleased. "I would very much like to try them."

"I'll take a pizza one so Hawk can try the breakfast ones," Cullen said.

"Okay, cool." Corbin stood and got a box out of the freezer. "And I get the broccoli one."

"Of course you do." Cullen gagged. "Ew."

"Stop it. Broccoli is so cool." Corbin put little frozen things in little paper tubes and then microwaved them.

How odd.

Cosmo chuckled. "Be careful what you let them talk you into."

"Are they not nice?" Hawk thought the boys seemed enthused for something that was possibly yucky.

"Define nice. They're kind of addicting, but nothing about them is actually food."

He didn't follow.

"They're yummy snacks," Corbin explained. "Not particularly nutritious."

"I thought they were breakfast."

"Careful, it's hot." Cullen handed him one when it came out of the microwave. "I'd wait a minute before eating it."

"Okay…"

"They're okay." Cosmo handed him a second one. "I want some fruit. That smells bad."

Hawk had eaten some truly awful things in the Middle Ages. This could hardly be worse. He tore one pastry open to look at the insides. Look at that. "So it's like a sausage roll."

Cosmo winced and backed away. "Yeah, no."

Oh dear.

Hawk bit into it and chewed thoughtfully. A movie line spoken about a bug by a lion came to mind. "Slimy…"

"But ugh." Corbin winked.

"I have had worse." It honestly wasn't bad. It wasn't *good*, but it wasn't bad.

"It smells like death." Cosmo was positively green.

"Oh, Cos, it's not that bad." Corbin chuckled. "I mean—"

Cosmo bolted for the bathroom, and Hawk handed Cullen his extra pastry so he could wash his hands. "We should have waited to call your mother."

"So, what part of this do you think made him urpy?" Corbin seemed more curious than concerned.

"The pregnant part." Hawk chuckled. "There's nothing wrong with it. But I can't eat more if I want things like kisses."

"Ew." Cullen rolled his eyes. "Well, I'm not worried about that."

Corbin rolled his eyes. "I was talking about feeding him like with food. Not kisses."

Suddenly, there was an odd sound, like the echo left behind after a bell stopped ringing.

About the time that Hawk recognized that something was coming, a willowy, sharp-featured lady with skin as green as leaf hoppers floated into the room.

That must be the mom.

She looked at both of her sons, nodded without a word, and turned her attention to Hawk.

"So, you're the one my son decided upon." Her voice

was surprisingly low, like two stones rubbing together. Fascinating. He'd expected light and airy, somehow.

"I am. He's my mate. I'm so glad to meet you. I'm Hawk."

"It suits you." She offered him an arched eyebrow. "Calla of the Flower Mound. Pleased." She held out one hand, and it was tiny but strong, and that reminded him of the triplets, all three of them.

He shook, careful not to squeeze too hard or to be too limp.

Honestly, he needed to check up on Cosmo. He needed to see how badly Cosmo felt, tell him that his mom was here already, because...

"Mom." Cosmo stood there just as suddenly as his mother had arrived, pale face a little damp. "I'm sorry, I wasn't feeling well."

"It happens to the best of us." She went over and kissed Cosmo's cheek, laying one hand on his belly.

Hawk could hear the ringing of bells, feel a vast rush of power, enough that it made his toes curl.

Hawk watched Cosmo as Corbin and Cullen went back to eating their Hot Pockets, while Calla basically stood there and glowed.

He wasn't sure if this was some sort of a fae ritual or what. Maybe he shouldn't speak—especially if she was doing some sort of magic.

One way or the other, the boys weren't giving him any clues on how to act.

She's blessing the baby. She's making sure all is well.

She's—oh, my love. My mate!

Yes. Cosmo began to laugh, the sound overjoyed, and it was all he could do not to rush for his mate, but he did stand, vibrating as he waited for Calla to let him swoop in.

She chuckled, the sound deep and earthy, and glided toward her other sons after kissing Cosmo's cheek. "Congratulations, my son."

"Thanks, Mom." Cosmo opened his arms to Hawk, who came to hug him close.

"Love."

"Yeah." Cosmo beamed. "We're pregnant. And it just took a Hot Pocket."

"Imagine that." Hawk couldn't stop grinning. Goddess, he adored Cosmo. And now they were having a baby.

Then she went to Cullen and handed him a package. "The mushrooms you requested, my dear. I love the way your house looks."

"Thanks, Mom." Cullen took the Hot Pockets and wandered off, muttering softly to himself.

Which left Corbin staring at his mom.

"Are we still fighting?" she asked.

Corbin shook his head. "Of course not. Thanks for coming. Cosmo needed you."

"He did. I'm glad to see him happy. You need to be happy too."

Corbin simply watched her and arched an eyebrow.

"I did bring you a gift." She handed him what looked like a handful of seeds, pouring them into his hands. "I found these. I don't know what they're for, and I can't make them grow. So I thought perhaps you could."

Corbin looked shocked for a moment, and then pleased. "Well, thank you. That was very thoughtful."

"I do love you, son. Even though we might snarl periodically."

Corbin nodded and rested their foreheads together. "I love you too, Mom. I'll let you and Cosmo and Hawk get acquainted and talk. I'm going to go see if I can't identify these seeds."

Then Corbin walked away, leaving them alone in the kitchen.

"Would you like some tea?" Hawk asked.

"I would, and I would love to see your home if that's an option."

Hawk nodded and smiled, tickled to show off. "Of course."

Cosmo smiled suddenly. "I would love to show you the house. We have the best bedroom, and there's a stained-glass window and a tower."

"And a nursery, soon?"

Cosmo nodded. "Overlooking Lunastra."

"Ah, yes. Well, that's—"

"Hawk was born there, Mom."

She looked stricken. "Oh. Oh, my dear, and now you're here…"

"With Cosmo. I will never regret that one bit."

And he meant it. No matter what else happened, he had a family now.

He would never be more grateful for anything than he was for them.

CHAPTER

EIGHTEEN

"I really like him, dear."

He was going to cherish that memory forever—the sight of his mother smiling, patting his stomach, winking at Hawk, and saying *I really like him, dear.*

Cosmo waved as she headed home, but he wasn't sad. She could come and go as she pleased.

He had to wonder about that, really. Why was it that she could come and go and the dragons couldn't? Were there dragons that could, and he just didn't know any? Were there fae that couldn't come, and he just didn't know any?

It wasn't like they had a lot of fae friends or anything. It just wasn't a thing. They hadn't been welcomed in polite company, sometimes...

But still.

He pondered that, because rules were important in the fae world, and he needed to know exactly what the rules were going to be for him and Hawk...

He needed to ask someone, but his mom wasn't the one to go to.

Cosmo really needed to ask his dad.

Not right now, though.

Right now was about him and Hawk and the knowledge that they were going to have a baby together.

Mom was gone, his brothers were in their respective houses, and he was alone with his mate.

Who, Cosmo thought, might just be losing his mind.

Hawk was pacing, talking to himself, and periodically looking out of the stained-glass window like he could make something out.

"You can't see out of that window. Love, what's wrong? Aren't you happy about the baby?"

It wasn't an honest question. He knew better. He could feel Hawk's nervous excitement. He thought maybe his lover just needed an excuse to talk to him.

"Happy?" Hawk blinked at him. "I'm overjoyed. I never thought I could have a child. I never thought I *would* have a child. I've been waiting for this moment for millennia, but now we have to decide all sorts of things. Where are we going to put the nursery? Is it going to be close enough? Should we move the bedroom? What about the stairs? There are so many stairs in this house..."

"I think we should put the nursery in the little drawing room we have here. That would be perfect for the infant stage, and then we move him downstairs—or her. I don't know yet. So don't read anything into that."

Hawk blinked. "Fine, not reading anything into that, but he's going to be amazing. Do you think that's big enough?"

Hawk couldn't be serious. "I could sleep in there. Yes, it's big enough. There's a *couch*."

"Well, I just want my child to have everything."

"He'll have everything." What was Hawk going on

about? This was supposed to be about snuggling and dreaming and being together. "Everything is fine. He has us. What more does he need?"

"I don't know, friends? A mate someday? To be able to go over to the dragonlands or to the Land of Summer? What will happen if he gets stuck here in this house?"

Cosmo blinked, all his excitement disappearing as if Hawk had blown out a candle.

He didn't know.

He just didn't know, and this wasn't what he wanted to start worrying about. They were supposed to be happy right now. They were supposed to be together and celebrating.

He didn't feel like celebrating anymore. "I'm going to go downstairs and make cookies, I think. Maybe we can watch a movie later. I'll be back in a few minutes."

He threw on a pair of sweatpants and a heavy sweatshirt, then padded downstairs as Hawk just stared at him like he was insane.

Cosmo sniffled, trying really hard not to simply burst into tears like an idiot.

He'd heard all these stories about how excited everyone had been when they found out that they were having babies —All of his friends from the Estes clan, the boss. Gavin, the bastard, had been over the moon even when things had been insane, when they were shifting over across the veil.

And then here he was, having a baby that he was possibly condemning to being trapped in this house forever.

Both Corbin and Cullen came running to him as soon as he hit the kitchen. "What's the matter?" they asked in unison.

"I don't think I wanna have a baby," he whispered.

"I thought you were excited?" Cullen said.

"What did Mother do?" Corbin asked.

"Nothing. Nothing, Hawk, just—What if he never gets to leave? The baby, I mean. What if he's stuck in here forever? He won't be able to find a mate; he won't be able to play with other kids; he won't be able to go outside in the sunshine. I don't want to have a baby. I hadn't even thought about that. I don't know what to do."

Both of his brothers stared at him, obviously stunned.

Then Corbin squeezed his hand. "Well, you don't know that that's gonna happen."

"Great, but I don't know that it isn't. And that's my job —to think of all these things—and I didn't."

Corbin raised a green brow. "Okay, but doesn't that mean there's nothing weird and portentous about it? I mean, we can go all over. Why can't he?"

"Because he's half Hawk's?"

"But he's also half yours." Cullen grabbed his hands. "It will be okay."

Mate? Hawk's mental voice was very careful. *May I join you?*

Of course. He sniffled and dried his cheeks. "Do I look okay?"

"Perfect." Cullen led him over to the sofa and wrapped up with him while Corbin got butter out, muttering about kicking Hawk's ass.

Hawk moved into the room, super quiet and shadow-like for such a big guy. He glided to a stop in front of the couch.

"I'm sorry, love," he said in a low voice. "I did not mean to upset you. There's nothing in my heart but joy." And

Hawk opened up his mind and let Cosmo see the jumble of emotions there: joy, awe, love. Need.

All for him.

He melted, but he was still going to make Hawk wait for forgiveness. Just a little.

"You made me very sad, Hawk."

"I'm sorry. I didn't mean to. I was a strategist once. A dragon who had to worry about dragon slayers. I think of all of the worst-case scenarios first so I can get them out of my system." That came with a wry twist of Hawk's lips.

"Well, that sounds awful," Cullen said. "Having to worry about people coming looking for you just to kill you."

"It was never pleasant." Hawk shrugged. "Times did change, at least."

"That's a blessing, I suppose, but... what if I—what if I'm dooming our baby? What if he hates me?"

"No." Hawk took his face between those big hands. "No, that could never happen. You are going to be an amazing father, my sweet."

He held Hawk's gaze, taking a deep breath. "I love you. I want everything to be all right."

"It will be then." Hawk smiled right into his eyes. "You're magical. I love you. That's what matters."

"That's right. We're going to make this baby so happy."

"We are. You and me."

Cullen let him go so Hawk could pull him to his feet.

"We'll be back for cookies," Hawk said.

"Peanut butter and chocolate chip in a couple hours," Corbin offered.

"Thanks." He gave his brothers a watery smile. "Really."

"Of course." Cullen patted the couch. "I'll have a spot for both of you for the Lego movie."

"Perfect. Go make up. We'll see you in a few."

Hawk chuckled, lifting Cosmo into his arms. "I make many mistakes, love. Forgive me? I was alone so long."

"I love you. I will always forgive you." He circled Hawk's neck with his arms.

"Thank you." Hawk carried him to their rooms, to their bed, which was what he'd wanted to begin with, and some of the joy he'd felt began to return.

"We're having a baby."

"We are. And I am so proud I could just burst."

"Oh that would be messy. You should knot me instead," Cosmo teased.

"What a capital idea." Hawk laid him on the bed and came down on one knee beside him. Then he took a kiss that curled Cosmo's toes. "I love you. I swear to you, I will make you happy."

"You already do."

"Good." Hawk rubbed noses with him. "Now let me make you really happy."

He laughed, arching under his suddenly very unworried mate. "Sounds like the best plan ever."

CHAPTER

NINETEEN

Hawk prowled his library, searching for just the right tome. He needed a book on dragon lore or fae law or something that would assure him his child would be able to be like Cosmo and go out into all the worlds his father might inhabit.

Just in case.

He had averted the crisis with Cosmo, which had been his own foolish fault. There had been intense loving, cookies, and movies, and Cosmo seemed his happy-go-lucky self again. Which was how Hawk wanted him.

But he needed answers.

He needed to know what options he had. There were so many questions—and he didn't know who to ask, but he knew he needed books.

So he gathered and stacked and wished there was a dragon librarian on call somewhere... Or a dial-a-fae. Oh, that was funny.

Maybe he needed to speak to Cosmo's mother. Surely, she would know how this worked...

Could he put in a call to her without Cosmo knowing? Not electronically, of course, but... Maybe through Bakli?

He wondered if his friend could help out.

"I do not have the answers you seek, friend." Bakli popped out of a book as if it were a door. "I am sorry."

"I've upset my mate, and it hurts my heart, you know?"

"I do." Bakli sat on the edge of the table, legs swinging. "Do you have any cheese?"

"It just so happens, I made a charcuterie plate." He offered the plate to his friend. "Please, make yourself at home. Have you heard the news? My mate is with child."

"Congratulations, my friend dragon! I am so pleased for you." Bakli smiled, his eyelines wrinkling up.

"Thank you, I couldn't be happier." Of course, that was a lie because he could be. He wanted to know how to fix this thing that he'd somehow, oddly, messed up.

Bakli took a piece of cheese in hand, looking almost meditative. "You worry quite a lot. It's not good for you, and it's not good for babies."

"I have the sinking suspicion there's a lot of worrying that comes with babies. Perhaps even more than just a little bit."

Bakli bobbed his head. "Yes, yes, yes, I understand, but..." He tilted his head, his hat almost falling off. "It seems a mistake to miss all of the wondrous magic that is happening for something as mundane as worry. Of course, it could just be me." Those bright eyes twinkled. Then Hawk knew he was being made fun of.

"Are you suggesting that perhaps I should be spending time with my mate instead of going over all these dusty books?"

"Yes." Bakli settled in, cheese in hand. "After we eat, of

course. Sharing the meal with a friend is also very important."

He took a piece of cured, peppered meat, snapping it out of the air. "I do believe you have a point, my friend."

Suddenly, his mouth was on fire, the heat both sharp and smoky enough his eyes crossed. A hint of smoke curled from his nostrils. "It's so good."

"What's good?" Cosmo came wandering in, wearing a huge puffy robe. "Oh, good day, Bakli. How are you?"

"Enjoying a snack with your mate. He was very generous to offer."

"And you were very generous to ask," Hawk teased. "Would you like some meat? The meat is very spicy," he warned.

"I don't mind spicy. The cheese, though—that smells good." Cosmo stole a piece of cheddar for himself, then he went to sit on Hawk's lap.

"Mmm. Hello, love." He was so relieved that Cosmo seemed to have forgiven him for making such a mess of things. He hated that he'd made his mate unhappy with his words and deeds.

"Hello." Cosmo munched his cheese. "Yum. This was a good idea."

"I agree." Bakli nibbled, sounding like a mouse, almost.

"Did Hawk give you our news? I'm going to have a baby. My mother came, and she let us know for sure. There's going to be a bouncing baby dragon—with a *little* bit of fae —bouncing around the house."

"I think that's glorious news. And he did. He shared. Hawk's very excited." Bakli chuckled. "I look forward very much to meeting your new child and to becoming his friend as I am his father's."

Cosmo nodded and leaned into Hawk, munching away. "It's going to be amazing. He's going to be amazing."

Bakli's smile was fond and barely amused. "Is it a boy?"

"I don't know. I don't know that he's decided, yet. I just say 'he' because it's easier. And 'it' just seems very impersonal. I suppose I could use 'they'."

"Whatever makes you happy. I will love the baby no matter what," Hawk said.

Bakli nodded. "As it should be. Do you know which room is going to be the nursery?"

"I think we're going to make the sitting room the nursery. You know the little room upstairs in our bedroom? When the baby's older, they'll take the next floor down. That's where the children's rooms could be."

"Could be?" Hawk felt his one eyebrow raised as if it had a mind of its own. "The children's."

"Well, yes." His dear Cosmo looked very sure of himself. "I can't imagine growing up alone. It's unfathomable."

Now that made total sense. Of course Cosmo couldn't imagine it. He'd never been alone for one moment, prebirth or after.

Hawk had been alone so long that sometimes he forgot to talk for hours. Cosmo would poke him, and in his head, he would think he'd said everything that was in his head, only to find out he hadn't even moved in an hour or more.

"I like that idea," Hawk said. "Children."

"Well, sure. Alphas love kids." Cosmo said that as if it made all the sense in the world as well. Maybe he was speaking from his recent experience with the clutches who had gone through the veil. "You don't have to have them. You just have to put up with pregnant omegas."

"I want to have all the children with you, my love." He

grinned. They would figure things out. That was his job as the alpha. And for now, Hawk was certain Bakli was correct.

It seemed ridiculous to borrow trouble and to not be able to enjoy his time with Cosmo, watching his mate's body change and enjoying the process. It was something he'd never done in all his long life, after all.

He was ready to have a new life, new experiences, a new family in every sense of the word.

Cosmo leaned on him, holding his hand. *Are you okay?*

I am amazing. So is the cheese.

Cosmo laughed, and Bakli gave him a broad wink, and Hawk felt... better. More centered. Less worried. Fate would give him what it would, and if he never got more than this family and this house?

He could be the happiest dragon who ever lived.

CHAPTER

TWENTY

ncle Cosmo. Come and play.

Cosmo had gone out to see the dragons and get some fresh tomatoes, kiss the babies, maybe see the boss, if he wasn't busy. Jules was pregnant again, and Gavin was busy becoming mayor of the town or something.

Regardless, Cosmo was craving fresh tomatoes, and the ones that came from the grocery delivery just weren't as good. It was winter in the human world, and everything was hothouse and just unpleasant, but he knew that Myk would have ripe tomatoes.

Uncle Cosmo, come and play. Kynan and Katrina—everyone called them the kibbles and bits—stood together, looking for all the world like exact replicas of one another, even though one was a boy and one was a girl.

They had given up their human forms altogether, it seemed, once the human world had been closed to them, and they sparkled, bright orange and floating without even moving their wings. They were a sight to behold in the sunshine.

"Kynan, Katrina, how are you? What are we playing?"

They twined their tails together, heads tilting, smiles almost vicious as they turned their gaze to little Stella, who was flying around Penny and Cali near the snapdragons. "Bite the changeling."

He waggled his finger at them. "You two be nice to Stella. I won't have that. That's not kind. What would your fathers think?"

They rolled their eyes and cackled a little bit. "You're supposed to be fun."

"No, not me. That's my brother. Cullen's the fun one."

In his head, he heard. *Yes, but you see things like we do. You see the things that will be.*

He could tell that they were used to overwhelming other dragons with their joint will.

But much like little Stella, who the twins were viciously jealous of, he did have access to the well of peace that somehow came with being partially fae.

"Mmm. I do. But that's not a reason to be mean." He held out his arms. "Come and don't bite me. I want to go get tomatoes."

Are you going to love your baby more than you love us?

No one loves us like you do.

"Oh, guys. Love isn't halved—I could never love you less."

They curled into him, and he poured out all his love to these two amazing dragons.

They sighed, leaning into him. *It's been so nice here, Uncle. It's kind of boring.*

He had to laugh. These two were used to a vast underground cavern that was their family's to explore. Village life might be odd.

"It is, loves? I bet you're right. Are there no exciting caves here?" He carried them through the sunlight.

"No. Not one. And there are such nice mountains behind us."

"Then there must be somewhere. You just need to get your uncle Ty to take you looking." Or Gavin. He had a talent for it.

"Can you take us?"

Oh, Hawk would love that... "I'll try, yes."

"Yay!" He got kisses on both cheeks.

"But not today. Today is for food."

"Tomatoes. Your—"

"—baby likes—"

"Tomatoes!"

"Yes, my beautiful loves! The baby likes tomatoes!"

"They're poison, you know."

He snorted. "Like Corbin hasn't told me that. Nightshades. Maybe my baby will spit poison like Austin."

Two sets of eyes went wide. "Ohh."

"Poison."

"We could teach the baby to spit."

"Poison. At whoever."

"We wanted them."

"To. And no one."

"Would know it."

"Was us."

He chuckled at them, stroking their scales. He and Myk seemed to be the only two who weren't a little bit worried about this pair. They weren't bad. Just powerful. And together, in a way that seemed very unusual to most people.

Cosmo didn't find it unusual at all. Their mother said he and his brothers hadn't spoken a single word that wasn't in unison for the first dozen years of their lives. They truly were one mind and three different bodies.

The twins liked to play that up. Naughtiness got them attention. It got them a little bit of shock. And it healed the wounds that were caused when other dragons didn't really want them.

Now if he could only get them to understand that in that way, Stella was sort of one of them.

"So where is Uncle Myk? Weeding the gardens? Or is he with the children?"

"Uncle Myk says his place is in the gardens. Growing things, and so he let us build our own garden. There's nightshades and wolfsbane. Foxglove. Hemlock. Jimson-weed. Mistletoe. Oleander. Belladonna. We promise not to use it. Promise not to share it. They said we could have a fence and a gate with a lock."

"Oh, that's very exciting. How grown you are to have your own special garden with such powerful plants."

Kynan nodded. "Uncle Myk trusts us."

Katrina agreed. "And we trust him. It's an agreement. And one does not break agreements."

"Very true. It's all about loyalty, you know, and trust. I would love to see your garden. But if you don't mind, of course, I'll stay on the outside of the fence. Because of the baby."

"That seems wise."

"Yes, wise, because we don't know what happens deep in the garden."

"We're taking classes. From a lady. The dragon lady. A witch. She's teaching us about new things. So you should stay out."

Now, that *was* a bit concerning. "But Uncle Myk gets to come in, yes?"

"Yes, Uncle Myk has the key to the lock, just like we do. That is also part of the agreement. Uncle Myk helps things grow. It helps things—"

Both the twins paused and put their foreheads together.

Uncle Myk knows about her. And tries to keep that away from everyone else. And that is good. We will never hurt him.

"That's because you are. Good. Because you care. I'm very proud of you both."

The orange turned a little rosy. And they wiggled around a bit, obviously pleased.

Jasper, who they called J-bot, came trundling over, the chunky little boy growing like a weed. This sweet lad grew out and then up and then out and then up. And he was going to be a tall, tall dragon. Cosmo could tell already.

"Uncle Cosmo. Katrina. Kynan. I was looking for you."

"You were looking for me? Did you know I was coming?"

"No. No, I was looking for the twins. But I'm glad to find you too. Uncle Myk says the strawberries are ready, and they're so good. And he wanted me to wait for you to make sure we all got some."

That earned another of those blushing little color changes. Then the twins were off and running. Heading toward the back garden with J-bot.

"Oh-ho, deserted so easily," he said, taking his own time to get across.

"Cosmo, is that you?" Egan waved at him, smiling.

"It is. I came to get more tomatoes. I heard that the vines were heavy, and there's nothing I want more. I feel like Rapunzel's mother looking for ramps."

Egan chuckled. "You look amazing. Sweet little belly. Come on in. There're strawberries as well. The children are about to have a party where strawberry fingers can't get on books."

"I understand."

"How's your mate?"

"He's good. He's been very busy. Reading and redoing the nursery and just being Hawk." Which was, he had to admit, an utterly wonderful thing.

"Ah, good. Good. I'm so happy for you." Eagan was a lovely dragon who adored tea and antiques and who always had a moment to chat.

"Thank you. Everything is well here?"

"Normal." Eagan winked. "The twins are...the twins. Arielle has been suspended from school. In the village. For three days."

"Fighting?" It had to be fighting, right?

"Insubordination. Apparently one of the teachers said something that could be construed as cruel to a small omega dragon and made him cry, and Arielle...went all Arielle, all over."

Cosmo winced. "Was there fire?"

"There might have been fire."

"Is she grounded?"

"She's up in the mountains with her father. Brand is teaching her the finer points of controlling one's temper as an alpha. If that doesn't work, we'll send her up with Tyson."

Cosmo wasn't entirely sure that Tyson was going to be the appropriate teacher for instructing Ariel about how not to lose one's temper and set the school on fire. But, not his circus, only marginally, his monkeys. "I assume Devon is here, and I can see him."

"Oh, he's most definitely here. He spent a few days in the library refusing to leave after Arielle pulled her stunt, but he's back to normal. I think that he finds it awkward being the father of alpha dragon children, but he's getting it."

"Arielle just has a fine-tuned sense of justice, that's all," Cosmo said.

Egan chuckled. "You are their champion. You three always have been since you met them, and the rumor from Sebby is that it's not just our Estes clan. It's all of the children."

He nodded. Of course they loved the children. They were, for all intents and purposes, good dragons.

"Well, I came to get tomatoes, and to see how every-body was doing…"

Eagan chuckled as Cosmo's belly rumbled audibly. "Now there are hundreds of tomatoes. You can take as many as you want, I think. Myk's been harvesting for you, in fact."

They walked around the house to this amazing court-yard. It was protected between the mountain and the houses so that it was a safe place for children to run and explore, and a wonderful space for Myk to collect water and grow his vegetables and fruits.

There were buckets of strawberries on a long table, and many of the children sat there, stuffing their little faces with the red fruit.

Myk glanced up at him, waved. "Cosmo, I had a feeling you were coming. I gathered some tomatoes for you. Still craving?"

"Always!" he laughed. "Thank you, my friend. The strawberries smell good, too."

"Happy day and welcome!" Sebby cheered.

The sun was shining, the children were bouncing around, and there had to be hundreds of them.

He thought that was an exaggeration, but he saw so many happy little dragon children in every color and shape and size. So many of them had found their forms at a young age. It was like watching a party of light. Pure joy.

He hoped that he had the same experience with his children.

If they could ever leave the house.

TWENTY-ONE

Hawk sanded down the cradle rails, then wiped them with a damp cloth to bring up the grain of the wood. The cradle, which he vaguely remembered being in his attic, had appeared not long ago in one of the rooms that had come to be in the center of the house. One of Cosmo's comfy rooms, he called them. The medieval-era piece had a lovely hood of carved wood, with panels set into the sides that had once had paintings of a dragon fairy tale.

Hawk thought he could recreate them with a little practice and care.

"What's all this?"

Hawk smiled over his shoulder at Cullen, who walked into the room carrying two steaming mugs of tea.

"A cradle for the little one."

"Oh cool, can I see?" Cullen handed him a mug of tea and kneeled down to look. "Oh, that's cool. Was it yours? Do you remember?"

"I remember having this. I don't remember being in it,

of course. Do you think that these cartoons were fairy tales?"

Cullen peered into the wood. "Oh, totally. You want some help painting it?" He held up one hand. "I mean, if this is like a dad thing, I don't have to help. I just sort of thought I'd ask 'cause it sounds like fun and we could hang out."

"I think that would be lovely. Thank you so much for the tea."

"You're totally welcome." Cullen crossed his legs and sipped. "Yeah, see. You can see the golden egg in this one."

"I would like to leave as much of the original painting there as we can and just fill in."

"I love that." Cullen grinned at him. "So we need to either figure out the fairy tale or make it up."

Hawk closed his eyes. "I can remember..."

"Remember?"

"My mothers singing to me about a dragon and a golden egg. It was stolen."

"Dude, you're not serious. Did the golden dragon go and eat whoever stole it and crunch their bones? Because that's what I would do. I would crunch bones—munch, munch, munch!"

Hawk wasn't sure that Cullen was actually bone-crunching material, but he let it go. "Let me see if I can remember." He tapped his temple with one finger. "How did it start?"

"Once upon a time."

"What?" He didn't follow.

"It's a fairy tale. Fairy stories start with Once Upon a Time. Everybody knows that."

"Okay." Hawk laughed and shook his head. "So, once

upon a time, there was a beautiful omega who lived in a tower, and the alpha came to woo her."

"Ooh, I like wooing. I like making with the woo. Don't stop." Cosmo came in, belly tight and round, a tomato sandwich in one hand and a cup of tea in the other.

"Right. Greetings, mate. Do you need a blanket?"

"There's one here on the back of the chair. Continue with the story, please. Wooing. You were at the wooing part."

"Is there going to be a lot of kissing?" The third of the triplets was heard from. Corbin wandered in with a sack full of willow branches for the basket he was weaving.

"Well, this is a children's fairy story, so the kissing will be limited at best. Are we all here now?"

"Yes, I brought cookies," Corbin said.

"So, you can totally stay," Cullen told his brother. "All right. Alpha dragon wooing omega in a tower? Go."

Hawk chuckled, settling in, his hand on the cradle, which was telling him the tale, he thought. "He brought her a fine casket of jewels. Some of the rarest fruits in the land. A stack of the most coveted books. But none of this pleased her. 'Bring me a golden egg,' she told him, 'and I will consider your suit.'"

"Attagirl. Make him work for it." Corbin muttered around a bite of his cookie. "You're going to end up fat and pregnant."

Cosmo put a hand on his belly. "Hey!"

"He's not at all fat." Hawk winked at Cosmo. "Shall I go on?"

"Please, mate." Cosmo licked tomato juice off his fingers.

"He adored her more than anything on earth or beyond,

so he searched the world for the mythical golden dragon eggs, which—"

"Dragons don't lay eggs," Cullen pointed out. "Do you think they used to, back in the olden days."

"I think it's because people associated dragons with snakes and lizards, so they thought we laid eggs." Corbin handed him a cookie to dunk in his tea.

It really was like having a trio of eager students at lessons.

He'd been a tutor once...

"Which had been fashioned by an ancient dragon during the classical era. There were four of them, and by all accounts, they had been taken to the four corners of the earth."

"Which is a sphere." Cosmo took a cookie.

"I think the point of this whole thing is that the alpha was just desperate to make this omega happy," Corbin pointed out. "It's all smoke and mirrors. Like she's asking how much will you do for me?"

"Does that make the omega a bitch?" Cosmo pondered.

Corbin shrugged. "Possibly, but you know he is asking her to get knocked up and carry a baby. He has to prove that he can provide, right? I mean, this is the olden days. Omegas were much less expected to be providers of their own, like for instance—us. We rescued people from being kidnapped and from vampires. We were fierce."

"What? What is this 'were' thing?" Cosmo pointed out. "Just because I'm pregnant doesn't mean I'm not fierce. I will eat your face. Someone tries to come in here that doesn't belong? Grr."

Hawk was not going to laugh because that would mean he wouldn't be allowed in the bed for at least a week.

And part of him did realize that Cosmo was fierce and had been this great warrior and was a guardian now.

But a huge part of him just saw his sweet, sexy pink, loving omega who was eating a cookie.

With his tomato sandwich.

Which was nasty.

Gooey and wet with white bread and mayonnaise.

Cosmo knew. Hawk could see the laughter in his eyes.

"At any rate, the alpha despaired that he would never find one of these great eggs, though he set off in search of the one told to be closest to his home."

"No traveling to distant lands for this guy."

"Oh, I think he did go." Cullen pointed at one of the cartoons carved into the cradle.

"He did. He traveled for years, chasing tales of the eggs from land to land, all the while sending letters to his omega love in her tower."

Cosmo frowned deep enough his forehead wrinkled. "I would think that she would want him rather than his letters. If you want letters and gold instead of your mate, that's not love."

"Maybe love was different then," Corbin pondered. "There were a lot more knights and plagues and things."

"Still, I would rather have Hawk than his letters. That's awful."

"Well, it's a fairy tale," Cullen said. "That means we're supposed to be learning something. There's supposed to be some kind of moral. What's the moral to the story?"

Corbin rolled his eyes. "We haven't heard the whole story. How the hell do we know? And why does there have to be a moral?"

"Because that's what these stories are for," Cosmo

pointed out. "I mean, they're supposed to teach little dragons things."

"Like omegas are big dicks who want big eggs?"

Cosmo's grin went wicked as hell. "I like big dicks. I cannot lie."

All four of them groaned in unison.

"I believe with this tale, we're going to find a very different outcome than just that." The rest of the tale came flooding back to him. "He nearly died retrieving the egg, but when he brought it back to the omega, she knew his love was true. She could trust him to protect their young. So she laid a hand on the golden egg, and a baby dragon unfurled from it, one with rare golden scales and the ability to heal all the wounds and scars the alpha had suffered."

He waited expectantly for the next round of commentary.

Instead he found them watching him, staring rapt.

"'I saved all your letters,' she told him. 'I waited for you.'

'But you made me prove myself with this gift. You do not love me as I love you.'

The omega was sad that the alpha felt slighted, and so she revealed to him what she had hidden before. 'I needed this golden dragon to heal me so I could leave my tower. Now I am free to go out into the lands with you and be your mate.'

The baby dragon curled around her, the glow from the two of them blinding the alpha for a moment. Then she rose from the bed he'd never seen her leave and came to him, putting her hands on his cheeks.

'Thank you for this gift. I am ready to be yours if you will have me.'

And the alpha realized that his gift had been about far

more than greed, so he took her away from her tower, and they made it their mission to keep the golden dragon safe as he grew."

"Oh, that's sweet," Cullen muttered, forming a golden egg between his hands, then letting it go in a shower of sparkles. "I do love a happily-ever-after."

"Why didn't she just say that she doesn't feeling well, and that she required help to get up and do shit? I don't understand." Corbin looked constipated. "Say what you need. Get it? It's logical and sensible."

Cullen glared at his brother. "Don't be a fucker. It wouldn't be a story otherwise."

"I'm not a fucker, you are. That is a story. It's a good story." Corbin waved his hands. "I need help here. How do I help you? Well, there's this egg that'll fix things. All right, I'll go get it because I love you. I really appreciate it. The end. Story. Beginning, middle, and end."

Hawk glanced at Cosmo, who was just sitting there, staring at him and crying.

Oh dear.

He stood and walked over to his mate, which drew the other triplets' attention.

"Oh no. What's wrong?"

"Cullen," Corbin snapped. "Don't flutter. He's hormonal, and he's got this thing about the baby never being able to leave the house, and Hawk never being able to leave the house. It stresses him out. We know this."

"The thing I love best about you?" Cosmo sniffled. "Is that you're so delicate."

Corbin rolled his eyes. "The thing you love best about me is that I don't lie. Also cookies. You all really like my cookies."

"Of course we do." Cosmo held up his arms to Hawk,

who picked him up and nuzzled his cheek. "Can we go have more? And can someone make me tomato soup?"

"I can make that." Hawk squeezed Cosmo hard. "I did not mean to upset you, love. That was the story I remember."

"No. I loved your story. Seriously. I just worry that I've doomed you."

"Stop it. No stress. It's bad for the baby. It's not good for you." He headed down to the common area.

"But—"

"I will kiss this mood out of you, you know." Bakli's words about enjoying this time kept coming back to him, and he was learning to tease Cosmo back into a good mood anytime he fell into sniffles or worry.

"Will you?" Cosmo's eyes went wide, but there was a blessed hope there. "Promise?"

"I promise, love. I want nothing more. After you have your cookie. But before soup." He would put the tomatoes in to roast and then steal his mate away for a make-out session.

"Mmm... a man who prioritizes food and sex appropriately." Cosmo purred and wiggled for him.

"I try, my love." He chuckled, because Cosmo was already drying those tears, smiling for him, and that was what he wanted to see.

His mate didn't need to be sad. He was no alpha in search of a golden egg.

Hawk had what he needed right here.

TWENTY-TWO

Cosmo wandered, reading a bit of a book here, eating an apple there. He was basically happy.

It was a beautiful day outside, both in the dragonlands and in the human world. On one side, it was snowing, and on one side, it was sunny.

The nursery was pretty much put together. Cullen had done an amazing job repainting the fairy tales on the cradle that had been Hawk's.

Hawk was happy and attentive, the baby was rolling and kicking. He felt healthy and solid.

All in all, life was all right.

Cosmo headed through the common area. Everybody was busy, so the rooms here were empty. Cullen was helping Mom with some project, Corbin was sorting seeds. Hawk was pretending to read while he napped.

Cosmo peeked at the rising bread and nodded approvingly at the stew that was bubbling on the stove.

Everything was just fi—

He stopped, swirls of diamonds seeming to sparkle

around his eyes, blinding him, and he stumbled forward, grabbing hold of the pass-through so that he didn't fall.

Uncle, Uncle, Uncle, Uncle, Uncle! The cry was wild and panicked, Katrina and Kynan truly scared and screaming for him.

Cosmo felt it everywhere, from the top of his head to the tips of his toes, this terrified screaming of his name.

Uncle, Uncle, Uncle, Uncle, Uncle!

He looked around in his vision, trying to figure out where they were. It was dark, he could tell that, and it smelled—not of rot, but of earth and of dank.

And it was cold. How could it be cold? It was summer where they were.

Uncle, Uncle, Uncle, Uncle!

I'm coming, I'm coming, I'm coming. I'll be right there. He wasn't sure where right there was, but he had faith in his vision and in the twins. He always did.

Cosmo heard a door opening and closing. Then he felt stairs underneath his feet, and he wasn't sure where he was going, but it didn't matter because he could hear them screaming for him, and he just kept walking down.

Down into the basement and then down farther and out and—

And suddenly it was dark, the vision was gone, and he didn't know where he was.

Faboo.

Okay, Cosmo, you can do this. He might not know where he was any more than the twins did, but he was a professional, and he knew what to do.

First, contact your team.

Brothers! The twins are lost. I'm underground. It's dark.

He wasn't sure whether they heard him, but all he could do was follow the plan.

He did love a plan.

He checked his pockets—a handful of hard candies, an apple, and a little pocketknife in one, plus a little notebook and a pen in his cargo pocket, and his phone.

All right.

He didn't have any service bars, but there was a flashlight. That was something.

All right.

Uncle?

Coming, dear ones.

You can hear us? He felt the relieved sobs in his soul.

Of course he could hear them. He knew he would find them. He would get them out because that was his job. He rescued people.

I can totally hear you, lovelies. I'm coming. Wherever they were, they had to be in the dragonlands, because they couldn't come into the house. They couldn't come through the veil.

So somewhere down here there was another opening. Something he would have to keep an eye on and be aware of.

Uncle, Uncle, can you still hear us?

Was that in his mind or was that in his ears? *Call again,* he thought. *But this time I need you to do it with your voices. Use your voices, dragons.*

"UNCLE!"

Whoa.

He did hear it. He absolutely heard them with his ears.

"I can hear you. You're going to be fine. Stay where you are. I'm coming."

Cosmo kept stumbling forward, hands held out in front of him because there wasn't a lot of light, even with his phone aglow.

This place didn't feel dragon made, though. It felt as if the ground was bumpy and rough, and he could hear the pebbles and gravel moving as he walked.

Can you two make light? Will you make light for me? Can you remember how to do that? Can you make light together? He felt their nervousness, their worry, so he kept encouraging. *Make a little light. I know it's hard.*

They weren't like other dragons, those two, but they had a spark.

Can you make the little soft light so I can find you?

He didn't want to trip, so he moved slowly, stepping carefully. He didn't want to hurt the baby, he didn't want to hurt himself, and he didn't want to go into labor. But this would be a terribly awkward place to have a baby, and it was a bit too early.

He saw a dim light coming from what seemed like forever away. *Is that the two of you? Can you see my light?*

Yes, Uncle. We can feel you. We can see you coming.

He should have brought a big flashlight and a rope and possibly a first aid kit, but visions were horrible that way. They never let you plan ahead with supplies like that.

At least when they'd worked with Gavin, he'd had a utility belt.

"Uncle! You're close. Come this way!" There was another sparkle, this one not a vision. No, this was the twins, their little light sputtering like fireworks. Or like very nervy fireflies.

"I see you. I see you. Can you see me?" He waved his phone.

There was a long tunnel. It seemed relatively narrow, heading straight for the kids.

He went right to them and held his arms open. They wrapped around him, shivering violently, their tails twining together and curling around his legs like they were boa constrictors.

"I'm not leaving. It's going to be okay. Everybody breathe." He circled them in his arms and held them close, tickled that he had on his hoodie. They could snuggle in, share warmth. "You're both so chilly. What on earth happened?"

It occurred to him, vaguely, that they weren't officially on earth, not here...

"We were exploring." Kynan's voice shook.

"We were exploring the caves."

"We wanted to see if we—"

"—Could find a way to you," Katrina finished.

"We miss you."

He let their twinspeak pour through him. "Did you tell anybody where you went?"

"No, everybody was busy."

"We were—"

"—bored. We wanted—"

"—to play. Everybody else—"

"—is doing things all the—"

"—time. So we were—"

"—wanting to do things, so—"

"—we came. And—"

"—we were exploring."

Cosmo tilted his head. "Why didn't you call your parents for help?"

"They didn't hear us." Katrina's eyes wheeled.

"You heard us."

"We knew you'd hear us."

He sighed softly. "Well, that is the truth. I did hear you. So. Do you know which way you came? Did you come from that way?"

He pointed back down the tunnel.

He wasn't sure whether to stay here with the kids and hope that someone found them, or to try and move. He hadn't done a lot of spelunking. He really wasn't the spelunking kind of guy. Neither were his brothers.

They explored houses a lot and periodically popped into caves, but this was *caving*.

It wasn't just like a hole in the mountain.

"Did you see anything wonderful while you walked?" *Did you see anything that could be a landmark*, he thought, but he didn't want to ask because he didn't want the kids to worry any more than they already were.

There was.

A pool that was filled with light. Kynan bounced.

A light pool.

A light pool? Well, how fascinating was that? "Well, could you—do you think you could find it again?"

Because Cosmo felt that, if there was a light pool, he could conserve battery. Possibly there was water that was potable. He had an apple. If there was water, there might be fish. They could make a fire maybe. Out of what, he had no idea, but this? That sounded better than Dark Hole, which is where they were currently.

We can try.

Everything is twisty.

And turny and small.

We thought we were heading—

Toward the house.

Their words ran together so that he couldn't tell who said what.

"Well. You ran into the veil, sweets. You can't go through. You know that, so that's why you got turned around."

But you heard us.

"I will always hear you. Your fathers are probably frantic. Can you reach out to them? Can they hear you?"

The twins closed their eyes, and their joined call was huge.

But Cosmo got what they meant. There was this odd echo like it was... a bubble.

"Hmm, a bubble. Let me try."

He called for his brothers, but it just echoed around them in the tunnel, and the stones began to shake, to fall.

"Rockslide. Fly, guys! Go! I'm right behind you!"

He shifted and ran, his hand holding his belly to protect it from falling stones.

The dust choked him, and the sound behind him was deafening.

His soul reached out to the one being it wanted most. His mate. *Hawk, Hawk, I need you. I have the kids and we're lost. I need you.*

A stone hit him on the back of the neck and the world went bright, then a deep, velvety dark.

Oh.

Oh shit.

He turned as he fell, and it was the last conscious thing he could do to protect the new life growing inside him.

TWENTY-THREE

Hawk was sitting with his book on his chest, dozing, when he heard Cosmo's frantic call.

Hawk! I need you!

He sprang to his feet, tearing into the hallway, where he collided with Corbin. "Where is he?"

Corbin held his head, hands over his ears, tears on his cheeks. "I don't know. I heard him, but it was such a weird, echo-y sound."

Cullen staggered toward them. "I heard him."

Hawk knew they weren't going to help him choose a direction, so he closed his eyes. *Where are you?*

He sent the call as loudly as he could.

There's a tunnel in the basement.

Hawk took off to the basement, his instincts telling him to hurry. He didn't bother to stop for supplies. He could make his own light, if need be.

When he reached the tunnel where he could scent his mate, he found Cullen and Corbin with him, so small and fast in their dragon forms.

The tunnel is blocked, Cullen said after zipping past him. *There's been a cave-in.*

Let me try to move it! Corbin also squeezed by him, claws on the rocks, his earth energy pulsing around them.

Corbin looked back at him. *I can't.*

Move out of the way. Hawk didn't think he could shift in this tight space, but his power wasn't dependent on his form any more than the trips' were.

He focused on the rock, finding the heat inside it, which there always was. The fire that had created it was always still a spark in the earth. Always. Rocks exploded into shards, and he protected the other two from them with his body, half shifted and ready for anything.

More rocks are falling. He could hear Cosmo. The mental voice seemed weirdly confused and off-center. *I have to take the twins. I have to run. There's more rocks falling.*

This wasn't going to work. *We have to find another answer. This isn't going to work. I'm causing more cave-ins.*

All right, we'll go the other way. They had to have gotten in some way. You just have to go find them. Corbin nodded once, firmly. *And we can get the rest of the dragons to help. The boss will help there. Their dads have to be frantic. Come on, let's go.*

Hawk followed without a question, racing behind the trips, and as he left the house, he shifted to his dragon form so he could fly after them, calling all the while to his mate.

Cosmo! We're coming. Where are you?

I don't know! We're running. I'm bleeding and the twins are scared.

They flew straight into an ant hill of hysterical dragons, all calling out and searching for the lost children.

When they saw him, they roared.

He roared back, because no one was keeping him from his mate, and Cullen flitted in front of him, easing everyone back. Making it clear he was there with Cullen and Corbin, he thought.

You need to stay still as soon as you're safe. I'm coming for you. He started examining the rocks and crags that rose sharply behind the houses for a way in.

Please. I'm a little worried. I don't have water...

We need to gather food and water. They don't have any. He snapped it at Corbin, who wouldn't get his feelings hurt, and who could coordinate with the dragons already here. Then he found a place to get into the mountain and had to shrink himself to zip inside.

He ran as if the hounds of hell were after him, and he heard Cullen following and reporting back to Corbin about where they were, how far they had gone. It got tight in places, but Hawk just muscled through, following his instincts and Cosmo's calls.

Two dragons he didn't recognize traveled with him. They didn't get in his way, for which he was eternally grateful, because his mate was down here, hurt, pregnant, and lost.

One of the dragons had to be the father of the twins because he could hear the panic in the roars echoing through the mountain.

The other dragon was just fast.

Large.

Focused.

Together, any boulders or obstacles they found they shoved out of the way, clearing a path.

We found it. We found the pool of light that the kids were talking about.

Good, good. I'm glad. He wasn't sure what that meant, but it didn't matter. Cosmo sounded happier.

What is this pool of light?

It's just exactly what I said it is. There's obviously an opening up in the ceiling. Way up higher than I can see. A shaft of light comes straight down and hits this water, makes it glow bright blue.

It's lovely and it smells sweet, but I'm not going to let the kids drink unless I don't have a choice. There is still stalactites and stalagmites down here. So it's a natural cave, a natural cavern.

Ah. That actually helped a great deal. Hawk was familiar enough with cave systems to know that if there was a pool, he needed to follow the water. The first part of the cave they had entered had been dry, which meant it had been in use by some sort of creature long enough to kill the rock. But now they were where it was damp, the sound of water dripping loud as long as the roaring stopped.

"I need to hear," he barked. "We must follow the water."

"We're with you." The huge dragon was calm, and he kept the other one steady with a hand on his shoulder. "Just lead on."

The caverns and tunnels twisted and turned, and on occasion, he had to crawl. This was wild, caving like he hadn't done in centuries, since he was young and full of piss and vinegar. That must have been how those children felt, as if they were exploring, like they were grand adventurers.

He would bet they were very sorry children now, or, if not, they soon would be.

Call to me, love. I need to hear your voice.

Everyone is getting a little fussy, Hawk. Including your baby. We're hungry.

I'm almost there. Somehow, he knew it in his soul. The

internal compass that would always lead him to Cosmo was pinging like mad.

He tried to breathe, but the air was like soup, and he knew he had to get Cosmo out of here. The way narrowed, but all he had to do was crouch, the big dragons behind him doing the same. He could hear them breathing, but the children's father had quieted as if he also knew they were about to come upon their quarry.

Call out to me aloud.

"Hawk?" The cry was still faint, but he heard it, and it gave him direction when the tunnel he was in split into two directions. He pushed a sizeable rock out of the way. The children would have been able to climb over it, but Cosmo's belly would need more room.

"I hear you!" he shouted, and he could feel the relief across the bond with Cosmo. Yes. Almost there.

He staggered when he burst into the cavern that held the pool of light, his vision graying out with the terrible brightness of it.

"Hawk!" The joy in Cosmo's voice was a palpable thing, and he was almost bowled over when Cosmo ran to him, flinging himself at Hawk.

"Papa!" He heard the cries of the children as they ran for their father.

"You came for me." Cosmo kissed his cheeks and chin.

"Of course I did, love." He pulled back enough to look critically at Cosmo, assessing his health. "Are you well?"

"Tired. A little wet. And hungry." Cosmo's belly rumbled as if to emphasize the point. "And a rock pinged off my head."

That explained the dried blood.

"We brought some provisions." The big dragon came up behind him, voice wry.

"Hey, Boss. Cool. Thanks for coming with Hawk."

"Rescues are my specialties. Hawk. My name is Gavin. Pleased to meet you."

"And I'm Eagan. These are my twins." That came from Papa Blue Dragon, who was holding onto the little ones like he'd never ever let them go.

"It's a pleasure to meet all of you. Was anyone marking our path?"

"I did." Corbin popped into the cavern, looking relieved. "Thank the goddess."

"Yeah." Cosmo sniffled. "Sorry, now that you're here, I'm a little wigged."

"You have every right to be, love." Hawk checked Cosmo over again, but aside from his bumped head, he seemed well. He put a hand on Cosmo's belly, sending a little call to the baby there.

Papa! The happy little thought suited him to the bone, and it was so much clearer than before.

He beamed at Cosmo. "Let's get you someplace safe, hmm?"

"Yes. But we need to explore in here later."

Much later, was his thought.

"No exploring. None." Eagan's growl was furious. "No children without adults in the caves. Do you two understand?"

"Yes, Papa."

"We're sorry."

"So sorry."

"Good. I mean it."

"Yes, Papa." They said it together, and they sounded truly contrite.

"Corbin. Can you fly up and see where the light is coming from?" Hawk asked.

"Of course." Corbin zipped up. *Minerals. The light is coming from the west, it's flooding in and reflecting off the crystals. I'll keep going, but they're beautiful.*

Don't go too far. I don't want us to be separated. I just wanted to know if that was a way out.

Doesn't look like it.

Then come back, please? "Looks as though we walk," he said.

"That's good. We need this clearly marked, and then sealed off," Eagan rumbled. "Thank you for finding them, Cosmo. You're my hero."

"You're welcome." Cosmo chuckled, but he felt the tension in that rosy body. "They called to me."

"You are the guardians." Eagan sighed. "Come on, you two. Let's go home."

"Okay." The twins meekly followed Eagan. Cosmo trailed after them, and Gavin smiled faintly at him.

"I'll take the rear just in case."

"Okay. This is—" The veil.

I'm sorry. Cosmo buried his face in Hawk's neck.

For what? You're staying with me. It wasn't a question.

I will. Forever.

Then it doesn't matter. Hawk really had no idea what any of this meant, but so be it. Wherever they were, they were mates. They would make it work.

They would raise their son in joy and community. No matter what.

CHAPTER

TWENTY-FOUR

What have I done?
What have I done?
What have I done?

He paced in the room that Gavin had given them, his eyes on fire. His head pounded where he'd been hit with a falling rock, and his belly danced a little with the baby kicking, echoing his agitation.

Hawk was going to be stuck here now.

And he was going to lose his mind.

His brothers were going to kill him, when he got right down to it. They were supposed to be guardians. The three of them. And he'd just messed it all up.

"Cosmo."

He jumped, almost slipping and falling. "Boss. I didn't hear you."

"No? I heard you." Gavin's voice was rich and familiar and fond. "How are you? You seem stressed."

"I am." He threw his hands in the air. "Hawk is trapped here now, and our house is out there." He waved toward the entrance to the house that faced the dragonlands.

Stressed didn't even begin to cover it, if he was honest.

He was scared. He didn't want to be scared. He wanted to be happy.

Gavin sat down in the easy chair next to the big bed. "How do you know he's trapped?"

"What? What do you mean?" He didn't follow.

"How do you know Hawk is trapped here? Have you tried to take him home?"

"No. No, do you think it'll work? If he can't, will it hurt him?"

"It shouldn't. I've tried." At his surprised look, Gavin chuckled. "You know me, kiddo. Say I won't. It just spat me back out here."

"Oh. I think he'll be happier if he can visit—here and his home, and I wanted you all to learn to love him."

"What can it hurt to try?" Gavin blinked at him. "You're really very pregnant."

"I really am."

"And you rescued the twins in the caves."

"I really did." He never even hesitated.

"You always were fearless."

"Not anymore." Cosmo put his hand on his belly. "But I had to go. They were so scared."

"Yes. Eagan's going to lock them in their rooms."

He chuckled. "I bet. They were also extremely contrite."

"Your mate went to seal up the cave entrance with Ty?"

"Temporarily, I hear, but yes."

Gavin nodded. "Smart move. No unauthorized exploring."

"No, they could have been terribly hurt." It made his heart ache.

"They're fine." Gavin rose. "So are you. Now, when your mate gets back, take a little walk."

"Right. Just try it. If not, I will live here with him. I love him."

"I can tell. And your brothers would be here and there as much as possible to be with you. In fact, new guardians might even be chosen." Gavin held up a finger when he would have protested. "Which is what leads me to believe that Hawk is more mobile than you think."

He tilted his head. "Oh. Oh, boss, that would be perfect. You don't know how I've worried about bringing a child into a house where it's trapped there. I want—I want him to know your babies. I want him to be able to play with Violet and Cordelia. And Leah and Esther. Ichi and Robin, Alex, all of them. I want him to know the twins. I want him to know Arielle. And little Sebby. Everybody. All the babies."

"You're going to give yourself palpitations or put your-self into early labor or something. You've got to calm down. Have you had some sort of a vision saying that everything was going to hell?"

The world seemed to stop at Gavin's words.

Then he saw it again.

The vampires.

The vampires are going to try to get through.

They're going to come through and try to infect the world. Infect all the worlds. What they've done was sunk into the house. And they want to come. And feed and feed and feed and feed.

His eyes were filled with crimson, and he couldn't breathe because there wasn't any air left, and he was gurgling, and the world was spinning and he needed to get out, and...

"Enough. That's enough. That's just enough." His brothers were there, holding his hands, and Hawk was there stroking his hair, and...

He was back where he belonged.

"Where did you go?" Corbin asked.

"I don't know, I was scared. Vampires are going to come."

"Here?" Corbin's eyes widened. "We fortified the house."

Hawk held him, then kissed his cheek. "We'll be ready for them, love. I vow it. We'll defend the lands. That's what you and your brothers are meant to do, and I am your mate."

It was as if the words wrote themselves in fire on the air. Hawk's immense store of magic swelled and burned, sealing the vow with a tiny flow of lava.

Cosmo had never seen anything like it, and as it winked out before it burned anything, he laughed, his chest feeling looser.

"You're amazing," he told Hawk. "I love you."

"I love you too. Together we can take on anything."

"And we made a baby."

"I'm going to barf." Cullin faked a spew of sparkling flowers.

Corbin chortled, grabbing one out of the air, and suddenly, it was a real flower. He handed it to Cosmo. "What do we always say? With us three, anything is possible."

He perked up. "You're right." He grabbed Hawk's hand. "Come on."

"What? Where are we going?"

"Don't ask questions, just come, and remember I love you!"

∽

Hawk jogged away with Cosmo, who was tugging him along like a small tugboat pulls an ocean liner. He didn't ask any more questions, however. He just moved down the stairs and to Gavin and Jules's front room.

Where there was an entire clutch of dragons.

"Uncle Cosmo!"

"Uncle Cosmo, you have to introduce us to your guy."

"You have to!"

"You need to!"

"You have to tell us who this is."

Little ones, mid-sized ones, big ones, all different colors. There were bubbles and bears and flying. And was that an owl?

Hawk blinked and just sort of stood there, frozen as he was absolutely and utterly surrounded in a rainbow of babies and gorgeous dragon magic.

"This is my mate; this is my mate. He is ours now. He is Corbin and Cullen's new brother and my mate. We're having a baby." Cosmo danced him about.

An amazing young lady with wild red curls and the barest spattering of black and red scales came up along with a rather large young man that had a very practiced stern face. "He's good though, yeah? You're going to be a good dad and a good mate. Right?" the young man asked.

"Cosmo chose him, of course. He'll be fine," the young lady snapped.

"You didn't even know him before now."

"Neither did you." Those red curls were tossed in a mass of aggravation.

"Yes, well…"

"And I'm older. I'm the eldest. I get to make the rules." She poked the boy's chest, making him grunt.

Another little girl moved up, riding a bear, and frowned

at both of the other two who were arguing. "This is *my* uncle Cosmo. He met *me* first. I am going to be the godsister of the baby, and this is going to be the godbear. Esther, tell them."

The bear, who was not small under any stretch of the imagination, turned to the other two and roared.

That sent all the other little dragons into a tizzy as they rolled and tumbled and fought to get to Esther and love on her.

The young lady threw her hands up in the air. "Children." Then she held her hand out. "I am Arielle Drake. I'm the eldest of the Estes Park clutch's children. I'm very pleased to meet you."

Hawk shook her hand, sparks traveling up his arm, but he ignored them. "It's very nice to meet you as well. And you are?"

The young man also held out his hand. "I'm Sebastian. Everyone calls me Sebby. She's mean."

One of the elder dragons chuckled. "Sebby."

"What? It's true. She's bossy and she always tells everyone what to do, and she always thinks she knows everybody and everything."

"That's because I do know everything. You were raised in a barn."

"Arielle." Another dragon nation was heard from. "Please be polite."

"Fine, you were raised in a very nice barn."

Cosmo cracked up. "Guys. He's good, I promise. Come here and hug me. I have to take him to the house. I wanted him to meet you all first. Of course I will be back, I promise. Maybe we can all have supper. Together, a big pizza party."

Do they have pizza here? Hawk asked.

If not, we'll order pizza and we'll bring it over. Trust me, they're not worried. It's not unusual for me to order sixty pizzas at a time. Cosmo's eyes sparkled.

Good to know.

"Can I come with you?" the girl on the bear asked.

"No, Lia. Next time, you and Esther can walk with me as far as the casita, okay?"

She pouted but subsided quickly when Cullen made it rain a shower of illusion stars. "Make a wish!" Cullen said.

Cosmo tugged at his hand, and Hawk followed, the dragons parting like the proverbial Red Sea to let them through.

Cosmo did take him right back up to the entrance of their house, where he stopped, looking uncertain.

"I'll go first," Corbin announced.

"I'll go second!" That was Cullen.

"We'll go together." Cosmo grabbed his hand.

"All of us." He glanced at Cosmo. "When uncertain, I find it best to do it at a run."

Cosmo laughed, the sound full of wild magic. "Then let's go!"

Together, they sprinted toward the door, three colorful little dragon elves and him, and whoosh. They were in.

They all four blinked, and then the triplets let out a wild cheer that was unlike anything he'd ever heard.

That was the fae in them, that wild light, that fire. He had never seen anything quite like it, but his entire soul responded to the sound.

Hawk added a roar to the commotion, because this was truly his home now. He knew he wouldn't lose it if he went into the dragonlands, and he would be able to live with Cosmo as they needed to live. As Guardians.

Together.

And their children would be able to have friends, family, a wide support group.

It was more than he had ever expected.

It was heaven.

"We need to order those pizzas." Cosmo's eyes were filled with tears, but there was no unhappiness in them. That was pure joy. "We have a party to get to."

TWENTY-FIVE

Cosmo was so happy that he could hardly bear it. He had to admit that he and Corbin and Cullen had even spent more than a couple of minutes making Hawk go in and out the door to the veil, just because. Not much. Only like ten or twelve times, just to make sure that it kept happening.

Arielle and Sebby thought it was the funniest thing they'd ever seen, their rare joint laughter filling the air. He was sure the twins would have loved to see it as well, but they were grounded.

Cosmo wasn't sure that they were even going to be allowed to come down and have pizza, and he was not going to get in the middle of that with Eagan and Ollie.

Nope.

Not his circus, only marginally his monkeys.

Besides, he had so many people to introduce Hawk to. Poor Hawk just seemed a little dazed.

Cosmo wasn't sure if it was the number of dragons he was suddenly being introduced to, the release of what had to have been a huge stressor, or possibly just a little bit of magical heartburn.

As Hawk successfully entered the dragon world again, Cosmo sidled over to his mate. "I think that's good."

"Yeah! Can we eat now?" Sebby asked.

Corbin's smile was fond. "Go take the pizzas to the table."

The kids grabbed the boxes and started heading up to the huge courtyard that the dragons had made. It was a place for the children to play, a common meeting ground, a picnic area.

It had been placed in a protected spot, but it was still far enough from Myk's garden that certain curious little ones couldn't go eat all of the tomatoes again.

Not that the thief could have been him, because he would never do that, but someone had eaten Myk's tomatoes without permission.

"How are you feeling? Are you excited? Do you want to go back? Are introductions okay?"

He wasn't sure what Hawk wanted, but he knew that he wanted his mate to feel as comfortable as he could.

"I'm fine just... I can't believe this. It's beautiful."

Cosmo nodded, looking around at the oranges and reds of the sunset, the green grass. "It is and so different. You can fly here for hours, and nobody's going to care."

"And so can our baby." Hawk's grin was huge. "I know you were worried about that."

"Yeah. It was the boss, you know, who told me that we'd better try. Because you know, you're here. You're a guardian too. A real dragon guardian. Maybe even more than me because I'm sort of a dragon slash fae guardian." Cosmo chuckled, but there was always that uncertainty lurking.

"Stop it. You're fine, you're perfect, and you're everything I need."

"Flattery will get you laid." Cosmo winked over, loving the smile on his mate's face. "So it's time for pizza and to meet everybody for real. You're gonna love the boss."

Gavin was one of the best men he knew.

Hawk nodded, the motion firm, solid. "He was determined to find you. That's enough. And we worked well together."

"I can see that." He drew Hawk to the picnic area, and they were surrounded in no time, a dizzying array of dragons vying to meet Hawk.

"Me!" That was the shout that rang out over everyone else, and they all turned to see Puck's little one, Robin, run over and grab Hawk's leg. "Up!"

"You, hmm?" Hawk bent to swing him into the air.

"Me, me," Little Robin cheered, those bright eyes just glowing, his arms held out like he was flying. Austin and Puck were watching with wide eyes. Utterly, perfectly shocked.

"Oh, will you look at that?" Cosmo breathed.

Little Robin was the shy one, and he never seemed to want to be with anyone but his dads, but look at this.

"Hawk, Robin. Robin, Hawk."

He could see Hawk's expression... just sort of melt. "Oh, he has a bird name too," Hawk said.

"He does. He so does."

God, Cosmo loved magic. He just loved how it made things happen.

He headed over to sit, his body heavy with the baby. "I can't believe how wonderful that is."

"Did you just see?" Puck chuckled. "I can't believe this."

"That's your mate, is it?" Austin asked, and he nodded.

"That's my heart. Isn't he beautiful? He's like Gavin and Zeke and Ty."

"He's huge. You know, I'm not the kind to feel insignificant, but damn." Austin shook his head.

Puck patted his mate. "You are everything. Absolutely everything."

Puck's words made Austin just beam. And he liked that, especially because he knew it worked when he did it too.

Austin was right, though. He had chosen a mate, or a mate had chosen him, who was easily as big as Gavin, possibly bigger, equal to him, and a guardian.

"And he's a guardian, and he can come back and forth."

The words just burst out of him, and everyone stopped for a moment, stared, and then began to chuckle and to congratulate him and Hawk, who was holding little Robin like he was enrapt.

Wasn't that a beautiful sight to see—Hawk holding a baby.

Soon it was going to be their baby.

He might just die right now of pure happiness.

Corbin wandered by and handed him a piece of pizza. "Eat. The baby's hungry."

"How do you know?" Cosmo asked.

"I'm your triplet. I know. Feed the baby. You know he's gonna like me best."

"I heard that," hollered Cullen.

"Now he's got a bunch of competition, too," Austin pointed out. "He could like any of us."

"Shut up." Cullen came over to sit by him. "He's going to love us all."

"Of course he is," Cosmo soothed. "He's my baby and you're my brothers."

Hawk swung Robin around again, and little scales and a

tail popped up on the wee one, his wings trying to sprout. God, that was cute.

"Fwy!" Robin shouted, and he sounded like a trucker, his voice taking on a bit of a roar.

The entirety of the dragons—top to bottom—went "Aww!"

Hawk smiled and flew Robin around. "Fly, little one! Fly so fast."

Lia patted her bear, and Esther tumbled her over, batting at her playfully. Thank goodness they had grown up together. And Lia was used to a little rough handling. Of course, there wasn't anything delicate about that little girl dragon.

Puck chuckled softly. Andy and Dustin had their hands full with that girl.

Privately, Cosmo thought it wasn't going to be Andy and Dustin who had their hands full. It was going to be Arielle and Sebby because there were three alpha children. All three of them were freaking fierce, and, well, most everyone had seen Arielle kicking Sebby's butt. Yet there was something about little Seb that was stubborn and utterly relentless. Like he was just going to continue doing his thing until he was done doing his thing. And damn the consequences.

Or really, damn Arielle.

Arielle and Lia, on the other hand, might just kill each other. And Lia had a bear.

Austin winked at him. "Don't stress it. There's plenty of room. And if push came to shove, those three would learn to work together. Like Gavin, Ty, and Zeke. They're convinced that they're the heads of everything. And they're working together." Mostly.

"I'm glad I only have to really deal with mine."

"Right now. Just wait until Cullen and Corbin mate." That was Hawk, who sat down with a plate of pizza in one hand and Robin tucked under the other arm.

Cullen gave Hawk a wide-eyed look. "Oh no. Nope. I'll be the perpetual uncle."

"And all I need to grow is plants," Corbin agreed.

"Easy enough to say that, but then when your mate comes along, you end up all starry-eyed." He glanced at Hawk as the baby kicked his belly hard enough to be visible to the others. "And then look where you are."

"Covered in goofy baby dragons!" Cullen teased, sending off a wave of fireworks.

"I love it." Hawk devoured a piece of pizza, sharing a little cheese with Robin, but soon he was covered, children climbing on him like a jungle gym to peer into his face and make themselves known.

Hawk seemed to be over the moon, his face blissful, and soon Gavin and Zeke came, sitting close so that the babies could climb on them as well.

"Where's Tyson?" he asked, and Arielle's father, Devon, rolled his eyes.

"Myk's pregnant. Again. It's unreal."

Cosmo's eyes went wide. "How many is this?"

"Seven, but three are adopted. So it's pregnancy number four."

"Wow." He put his hand on his belly. "I can't even."

"I know." Devon's grin was totally conspiratorial. "Arielle and Jasper are enough, especially now. There's so much here to explore. This is a whole new way of life, and we have two more families in our little clan now. I'm actually building a store in the village with Ollie. We're remaking Marks and Reaver!"

"Oh, wow. You have such a library. And I can keep

looking on the other side for you, if you want. Or Cullen can, I guess. He's better with the online sales auctions."

"That's it. We're going to be careful, though. I don't want to destroy the culture. I want to become a part of it, you know?"

"Sounds good. You just let us know what, if anything, you need."

"We will." Devon beamed at Arielle, who was passing out pizza like a little matron at an orphanage.

"So has she made any friends down in the village?" Cosmo basically remembered that there had been a girl-friend that Arielle was desperate to see back in the winter. Someone with a merman best friend if he recalled correctly.

"Oh yes, Siren. She's quite charming, even if her parents are a bit... concerned with her dating. 'Her' being Siren, not Arielle, who would like to be known as Sparkle." Devon rolled his eyes. "Sparkle. Because that suits. At any rate, Siren's parents are very concerned about their amazing daughter dating someone who's, you know, a mountain dragon.

"A mountain dragon." He blinked, not sure what to think of that.

"A fire breather even." Devon lowered his voice. "This is where you clutch your pearls."

"Pearls. This is the one with the merman best friend named Bubbles."

"Yes."

"So the pearls is a pun?" Cosmo teased.

"Yes," Devon deadpanned.

"So how's the rest of this whole thing going?"

"Well, besides the Sparkles thing, Siren is actually quite sweet and dear and gentle, and we all adore her. We have not yet met Bubbles. We have met the parents. Not Bubbles's. Siren's."

"Is it always this confusing?" he whispered. "This is a lot of names."

"I'm assured by everyone in the village who has more experience with teenagers than we do because she's our first, and the oldest, that this is all perfectly normal, and that yes, it's always this confusing. Apparently, she's acting in a way that is appropriate for her age. And so I am trying to be Zen."

"I think they're right. I mean, Arielle's not the most humble child on earth to begin with. I think she's trying very hard." Brand sat down with a thump. "Either trying very hard or trying very hard to be trying. There was a really cool little wordplay in there, and I just missed it, but you know what I mean."

Cosmo had no idea what Brand meant, but he nodded. "Like working hard or hardly working, right?"

"Exactly. Thank you. I appreciate it. Is there more pizza?"

"Your daughter is doling it out."

"Yo, Sparkles," Brand called. "I want one with sausage."

"On it, old guy."

"I'm not going to kill her. I'm not. Not at all. Even though I'm fairly sure that she's the one who recently attempted to give J-bot a robot tattoo."

"Ouch." Hawk chuckled. "That seems extreme."

"She's always been a little extreme with her brother," Brand said with a world-weary air.

"This is what you have to look forward to," Devon put in.

Hawk just nodded down at little Robin. "I can't wait."

"Are you okay?" Arielle came over with pizza for her dad. "And I'd like to be perfectly clear, I did not try to tattoo anything on him. I was practicing making leather art. He got in the way, and he got the burning stick in his arm and it left a dot. Don't exaggerate and make me sound worse than I already am."

Brand nodded to her, face a study of patience. "You know what? You're absolutely right. I was just—"

"Trying to be funny. I get it. I totally get it, but everybody already thinks I'm an asshole."

"You don't have to make it worse, Arielle." Devon's voice was deadly. "Your father said he was sorry."

"Right on. Does the baby want another piece of pizza?" she asked Cosmo, and he nodded eagerly.

"The baby is always into pizza. The baby is always into eating anything with tomatoes—fresh tomatoes, tomato sauce, ketchup. It doesn't matter."

"Tomato soup," Brand offered.

"Tomato juice," Devin teased, and Arielle wrinkled up her face.

"Tomato aspic."

Cosmo blinked at her. "How do you even know what an aspic is?"

She rolled her eyes. "Siren's parents invited me to supper, and they had one. Oh man, talk about nasty."

Cosmo grinned at her. "Did you eat it?"

She nodded her head. "Sort of. I mean, I poked at it a lot with my fork. It moved. I think perhaps it was a living thing, and they were trying to get me to put it in my mouth."

She looked at Brand, winked at him. "The good news is I didn't offer to set it on fire."

"That's my girl." Brand grabbed her by the waist and

hugged her real quick. "Now feed your Uncle Cosmo's baby."

"Then can you give one to Hawk as well too?"

"Sure." Arielle leaned down, whispered. "What does he like?"

"He likes all the meats."

"Ah, a dragon after my own heart." She winked and headed off, which was when Sebby joined them.

Like the changing of the guard.

"Did anyone need more pizza?"

"Arielle is making rounds, kiddo."

"Ah." He gave a very cat-with-cream smile, as if he'd known that, and sat down, smiling at Hawk. "It is very nice to meet you, Sir."

"And you as well, Sebastian. I have heard a great deal about you."

"Thank you!" Sebby beamed at him, and Cosmo chuckled. Sebby never even considered that someone would say something bad about him and mean it.

There wasn't a lot bad to say, come to that. Just that he was competitive with Arielle.

They were firstborns, fierce and strong and loving.

His son would be their firstborn. How cool was that?

It's better than cool, mate. It's amazing.

He nodded at Hawk. *It is. I love you.*

I love you too, my own. You have given me everything.

They leaned together, noses rubbing together, and little Robin joined right in.

"Luff. Good luffs."

TWENTY-SIX

Hawk loved being able to go out in the front of the house as well as the back. The only direction he couldn't go was to the Land of Summer, where the fae relatives were.

He'd tried. He just ended up back in the house.

That was all right.

He didn't mind. He had the opportunity to make trades and friends with the others, and he felt... satisfied on a bone-deep level. And when it was time to meet his father-in-law, he had no doubt they could arrange it in the house somewhere.

They would be able to get him in and out.

Or meet him at the door, if need be.

Regardless, he was hunting his mate, who didn't seem to be in the house.

He had to be in the house. He'd promised not to go out to either land without someone—Hawk or one of his brothers.

Mate?

Hmm?

Where are you?

In the basement.

The basement. Just where his hugely pregnant mate should be.

Why?

I'm curious.

Hawk headed for the basement, talking as he went to try to triangulate Cosmo's location. *About what?*

Whether or not the cave-in blocked everything.

So... you're down in the caves where there are falling rocks?

Nothing is falling at the moment...

Oh that was too damn coy. He hastened his pace, because if Cosmo got stuck in there, Hawk was going to spank him, pregnant or not. Fear made a great motivator.

What's wrong? That was Corbin, the eldest brother so damn sensitive.

Cosmo is in the basement. Where the cave-in is. He wasn't above tattling if Corbin was closer.

Oh, that little shit. Cullen and I are with Mom. She's making a baby buggy.

I'll find him. He would, too. And if he needed help, he'd call to the dragons on the other side. Or see if Bakli or the gnomes could assist.

Holler if you need me. I'll be right there.

Thank you.

He reached out for Cosmo again, trying to make sure he was still okay. He heard humming. Cosmo was clearly in a good mood, at least.

He headed down into the basement, following the sound of his lover, who was wandering and moving rocks.

"Cosmo..." he called out softly, wondering if he should have brought cookies as a lure.

"Here, love." Cosmo's pleasure wrapped around him like a hug.

"There you are." At least Cosmo hadn't tried to crawl into the narrow tunnel.

"I wanted to see how bad it was. See if I could get through."

"Well, I think that's a monumentally bad idea. Let's tie Cullen to a string and send him."

"Yeah?" Cosmo chuckled softly. "I'm a little bored, you know?"

"All you had to do was say so, love. I would have found something to keep you busy."

Cosmo rolled his eyes. "Would you now? And how would you keep me busy? My great big old dragon."

"Old?"

"Ancient."

"Now you're just being mean." Hawk leaned down and rubbed noses with Cosmo. "Come back up into the light, love. It's... it's dark down here."

And he wanted Cosmo out of these caves. There were just so many opportunities to get hurt or lost or over-wrought or something. He wanted his pregnant mate not down underneath the ground.

This was not unreasonable.

"Okay, I'll come with you." Cosmo rubbed his belly, stretched. "Your son is heavy. He's very heavy today."

Hawk wisely did not point out that was because Cosmo was the size of a house. He thought that would go over poorly. "Is he going to be a big bouncing baby boy?"

"I think so. Our Elliot is going to be amazing. On the order of Arielle and Sebastian and Lia."

"You know you've cursed him now to be—" He stopped,

and his head tilted. "Honestly, as far as being difficult children, Arielle is the top."

"You only say that because you haven't spent as much time with the twins."

Hawk grinned. "Which ones?"

That cracked Cosmo up. "Well, I was talking specifically of the special Ks, but point taken. You know how we multiple children—"

Cosmo stumbled on a loose bit of gravel, almost falling, and it was all Hawk could do not to just growl and say, "See? This is why I didn't want you down here!"

It wouldn't help, so he didn't do it. He absolutely wanted to though.

"Can we stop for a minute?"

"I'd really like to get you upstairs," Hawk answered. "It's not very much farther. I could carry you."

"My back hurts. I just need to take a second and rest, all right?" Cosmo's frown was deepening, and that worried him.

"All right, of course." He wasn't going to argue.

If the pain kept getting worse, he would just carry Cosmo upstairs, dammit.

There had been a lot of talk about their baby being born over in the dragonlands where there were midwives and professionals, but Cosmo was absolutely unmoving about this particular subject.

Their baby was going to be born in their home.

Corbin insisted that he had read and trained and practiced. He had even bothered to go and attend births in the dragonlands with other midwives just to make sure he wasn't going to do any damage.

Hawk guessed that Eagan had done it the first time

without anything, so if Eagan could do it, then so could Corbin.

Eagan was a little... fussy.

"Are you ready to move on?" Something was in the air. Hawk could taste it. He wasn't sure what. But it was urging him to get Cosmo to safety. His protective instinct was on high alert.

"I—" Cosmo looked up at him. "Help me?"

"Oh, love." He lifted Cosmo gently, and then he hastened to get him back up to the house.

"Don't feel so good." Cosmo clung to him, fingers digging into his shoulders.

No, no, he could tell. He had to move faster now. *Corbin, I think something might be wrong.*

What, did the rocks fall?

No, no, listen to me. Cosmo doesn't feel—

Cosmo cried out a sharp, hard sound of pain. And then? Hot liquid seemed to just pour from him.

I think my water just broke.

I think so too. In fact, he would lay money on it.

His water just broke. I think we need towels. And sheets and hot water. I'm sure hot water needs to be involved. Hawk babbled, not wanting to do this alone.

Hawk. Chill. Where are you? Was that laughter in Corbin's voice.

Hawk realized that he wasn't sure that he knew. He was walking, and they were heading up somewhere in the basement.

Oh my. A light. It appeared like magic at the top of the stairs. And there was Corbin, staring down at him. *You're in the basement, dear. Come up. Let's get you cleaned up, all of you. All right? Cullen's getting the bedroom ready for you.*

Cosmo smiled at Corbin, the expression a little pained. "I don't feel so good."

"That tends to happen when you're in labor. Well then, we get you in the bathtub. Water's supposed to help." Corbin looked at him. *And you? I expect you to get your shit together. Sooner than later.*

Hawk nodded. *Yes. Of course.* He was a dragon of action. He could do this. His mate was in labor. His son was coming.

"Are you mad, love?" Cosmo asked. "Don't be mad."

"How could I be angry, sweet? You're having a baby!"

Cosmo took a shaky breath. Let it out in a huff. "We are. Elliot's coming. I hope he's not pink."

"What? Why? You're beautiful. You're perfect. Why, I would love if he were pink."

"No, no, I don't want him to be pink. I want him to be just like you. I want him to be perfectly beautiful." Cosmo began to cry. Hawk told himself this was hormones. That and a touch of fear and some pain, and not to panic.

It was all a lie.

He was panicking. He hustled Cosmo into the bathroom. He got him stripped down and into a tub of hot water. Thank you, Cullen.

As soon as the water wrapped around Cosmo, he seemed to relax. The pinched look on his face fading.

"What can I get you? What do you need?"

"You? I need you. Also possibly some apple juice. But mostly you."

Hawk smiled, and he remembered what Tyson had told him, the big patriarch of the Estes clan. Tyson had looked at him, smiled, and said, "Remember. Every single baby that you have, this is the only time that this will ever happen. This is the only time this child will be born. Pay attention."

So he fought to do just that. He petted Cosmo and praised him, letting him know he wasn't alone. That he was special.

"Hawk. Hawk, it hurts." Cosmo clung to him, a little panicky.

Hawk wasn't sure what to say to that. Possibly, "You're in labor." Probably, though, he should just keep his mouth shut. "If you want me to rub your back…"

That was when Cosmo shook his head, and then nodded again. "This is less fun than advertised."

Corbin tilted his head. "It was advertised as fun?"

"No, asshole, that's the point!"

Those words were sharp enough, Hawk supposed. Corbin just laughed. "Good to know. Next time, don't get pregnant."

"I'm not going to let you be Elliot's favorite if you don't be good. And stop torturing his father."

"I'm only torturing one. I'm being nice to Hawk." Corbin dropped a kiss to the top of Cosmo's head. "I love you. It'll be over soon, and then you'll have your baby in your arms. Try to focus on that." Then Corbin offered Cosmo another grin, this one much more wicked. "Or you could just focus on how you want to castrate Hawk. That works too. One way or another, there's going to be a baby."

"Elliot." Cosmo blew out a hard breath. "His name is Elliot. Can you hear him, Hawk? Myk told me that. Tyson could hear the babies. Gareth said that Zeke actually called the babies out. Can you do that? Can you talk to him?"

Hawk had heard the little burbles and laughter and joy inside Cosmo. Of course, he hadn't done more than to just enjoy the sensation. He didn't want to interfere with the child's growth process, after all.

But if Cosmo wanted him to try, he would.

Elliot? Can you hear me?

There was a pause, then a bolt of curiosity like lightning.

"I think he's listening." *Hello, love. It's your papa. I want to meet you.*

"Of course he is. Tell him it's time, hmm?"

"I'm working on it." He smiled at Cosmo. "He's curious. He wants to meet us too."

Papa? That was the tiniest whisper in the center of his brain.

Oh. He nodded, tears stinging his eyes, smoke curling from his nose. *I hear you, son. Come on out now.*

A little buzz of worry answered him, then a rush of what he could only describe as determination.

Da is ready for you. He's tired. He cradled Cosmo to him, loving on him, nuzzling his neck.

Da. Another rush of will. Their son was going to rule the world.

"Yes, sweet. Da and I are ready. Come on, then."

"Good job, guys. I see his head. We've got baby head!" Corbin sounded stupidly excited.

"Oh, thank the goddess." Cosmo tried to breathe, but he was red-faced and looked like he was in agony.

"I have you, love. I have you both." And he swore, then and there, that he would spend his life making theirs good.

"Love you." Cosmo gasped it out, and that birthline... Goodness, it was splitting.

"Push! Push, let's do this!" Corbin was there, ready to catch.

"Okay." Cosmo whooped for air, and Hawk chanted his name and Elliot's while Cosmo pushed. He was working so hard. Doing so well.

It took forever and absolutely no time at all before it was over, Elliot screaming in his uncle's hands.

"Oh, loves. You did it." He wanted to laugh. To roar. He whispered it.

"Our son." Cosmo stared, his eyes wide. "Our son."

"Yes. Elliot." He stared at them, because Corbin had cleaned Elliot and handed him to Cosmo.

"Help me, Hawk. Close up the birthline with your heat when I tell you."

"It won't hurt him?"

"Eagan says it's natural as breathing. Don't worry."

"You can't hurt me, love. You're my mate." Cosmo's utter faith gave him the impetus he needed, and he reached out, sealing the birthline with some of his internal fire.

The sight of his mate, holding this healthy little baby, his scales a pale, silvery gray, made him smile.

"Look at you both," Hawk breathed, as proud as any dragon could ever be.

"He's beautiful. Our boy." Cosmo's sigh was utterly satisfied. "Our baby boy."

"He is."

Papapapapapadadadada.

"I can hear him." Hawk was ecstatic.

"So can I." Cosmo laughed. "They can probably hear him in the dragonlands."

"That's a lovely thought." He sighed softly, shaking his head. "You're beautiful. You're so beautiful, Cosmo. Thank you."

"I love you." Cosmo held Elliot close and closed his eyes. "But I'm tired now."

"I'll watch over you, love. I promise. I'll keep you both safe."

"I know. I believe you. We're your clan."

"You're my family." And that he would never lose. Not now.

Cosmo had made him a believer.

TWENTY-SEVEN

"Corbin, Cullen! Come say hi to Dad." Cosmo laughed, looking out the door at his father, who stood where their house met the Land of Summer.

He wanted his dad and Hawk to meet face-to-face and for his mom and dad to meet Elliot before they headed to the dragonlands to show him off to everyone else.

"Can I hold him, son?" Mom's eyes were filled with tears. "Our first grandchild. He's perfect. Absolutely perfect."

Dad nodded, handing him a beautiful carved dragon.

"Oh. Wow. Thank you."

"For his nursery. It is good to meet you, Alpha Hawk. What clutch are you from?" Dad bowed to Hawk.

Hawk bowed back. "The Lethiel clutch of Arasma."

Cosmo blinked. He'd never heard Hawk say anything like that.

"An honorable clutch. Our family joins with yours in pride."

"Thank you, sir. I am pleased to be a part of this family, as well. And of the Rocky Mountain clutch, newly formed in the dragonlands." Hawk's face was just wreathed in smiles.

"Ah, I have heard tales."

He handed the baby to his mom while Corbin handed gifts to dad. "Hey. I did it, Dad. I played midwife."

"You have always been wise with growing things, son."

Corbin beamed, and Cullen rolled his eyes.

He's never going to get his big head through the door...

But he's so happy. I can't even tease.

Daaaaaaa. Elliot was just singing in his head as he played with Mom's nose.

"That's your grandmother, son. Your grandmother and grandfather." And soon they would meet Gavin and the other dragon children. Soon.

Hawk glanced over at him. *So many wonders to teach him. Thank you, love. For all of this.*

You came to me. You found us. You came home.

I did.

Hawk had waited so long, but Cosmo was grateful he had. He couldn't imagine his life without his mate now.

"Hawk just wanted to meet you and let you meet Elliot. I'll come back with him later today, okay?"

"Of course. Go fly him to the village and show him off." Mom handed the baby back, sniffling. "Tell the dragons hello from us."

"I will. Love you both!"

"Love you. Corbin, come back and let me show you some new cuttings later as well."

"And Cullen, I have things to show you in the shop."

"Okay, Dad." Cullen winked at him, and Cosmo chuckled.

Look at us all getting along, Corbin said.

I think we're going to need to. An echo of a prophecy floated through his mind, but he pushed it away.

No visions right now.

He had a baby to show off with his mate.

End

WANT MORE?

Join the Spurs and Shifters Newsletter for free stories, news, and contests from Minerva Howe!

Or check out my Patreon for exclusive news and stories!

Also by Minerva Howe

Dragon Veil Universe

Dragon Hoard

Dragon Scholar

Dragon Collector

Dragon Treasure

Dragon Prophecy

Mist Dragon

Cloud Dragon

Shadow Dragon

Dragon Sanctuary

Winter Dragon

Ice Dragon

Frost Dragon

Snow Dragon

Frozen Dragon

Misunderstood

Wolven Winter

Shifting Winter

Healing Winter

Solitary Dragons

Archer

Aiden

Devlin

∽

Heartstone Rescue

Mending the Dragon's Heart

Healing the Dragon's Heart

Catching the Dragon's Heart

Forging the Dragon's Heart *standalone novella*

∽

Mated at the North Pole

Rudolph

∽

Mated to His Reindeer

Love at Frost Bite: Cupid

∽

Moonlight Mountain

Chosen Wolf

Found Vampire

Broken Wolf

∽

Planet Fantasy

Completely Alien

Space Pirate Playtoy

Rocky Mountain Java

Coffee and Honeybuns

Decaf and Bearclaws

Secret Springs Universe

Home for…

Home for Ryan

Home for Stone

Home for Charlie

Secrets Springs

Pens and Needles

Halos and Heroes

Fire and Ice

Pride and Power

History and Haunting

Secrets Springs Healing Hands

Bad Boy and a Baby

Oro Escondido

The Billionaire Dragon's Sweet Mate

Alpha Triplets

Hunter's Moon

Thunder Moon

Wolf Moon

Alpha Triplets Box Set

Dragon Triplets

Dragon of Fire

Dragon of Glass

Dragon of Passion

Gryphon Triplets

The Gryphon's Jewel

The Gryphon's Prize

The Gryphon's Dragon

ABOUT THE AUTHOR

Minerva Howe is the kinky alter-ego of Julia Talbot. She lives in the great Southwest, where there is hot and cold running rodeo, cowboys, and everything from meat and potatoes to the best Tex-Mex. A full-time author, Minerva is a hybrid author. She believes that everyone deserves a happy ending, so she writes about love without limits, where boys love boys, girls love girls, and boys and girls get together to get wild, especially when her crazy paranormal characters are involved. Visit Minerva's website at: minervahowe.com